STONE COLD HEART

(FAMILY STONE #1 JESS)

LISA HUGHEY

STONE COLD HEART

by Lisa Hughey

December 2013

Lisa Hughey

ISBN: 978-0-9840428-6-9

 Created with Vellum

To my family.

CHAPTER 1

In the early evening dusk, Jess Stone lay on her stomach in the twenty foot high rubble of a demolished church, underneath a black and gray city-scape tarp intended to camouflage her position. A sharp-edged chunk of debris dug into her lower rib cage, the scope of the Remington M24 cool and familiar against her face.

Her standard uniform of jeans, running shoes, and plain black t-shirt rendered her just another anonymous and transient relief worker...which she was actually. A black baseball cap hid her distinctive multi-hued blonde hair. The paper mask kept out the contaminated dust from the destroyed buildings but did little to stem the overwhelming stench of decaying bodies.

Tanks rumbled through the destroyed coastal town, their public address system blasting warnings for citizens to stay in their homes, curfew was in effect. The threat was a joke. Ninety percent of the people in the town didn't have homes left. Those who did were terrified to go back inside. In the fetid, humidity choked air, the tent cities erected in the parks

1

and on the beach were seething masses of the injured and shock struck.

The substandard construction in the small country had never been enough to withstand the angry might of Mother Nature. Buildings had toppled like a stack of Tinkertoys, and left crumbling cement walls with twisted rebar poking out of the jagged ruins like a skeletal hand.

Trapped in the concrete pieces that littered the ground, the heat from the tropical day seared through her thin sturdy clothing. The stank of the raw sewage that ran in rivulets through the streets overpowered the salt-laden breeze off the ocean. People, covered with the grit of pulverized buildings and humans, shuffled along with blank vacant stares. Two weeks after the quake, still in shock, their lives decimated first by nature and then kicked and beaten by the ineffectiveness of a flawed relief system. Hundreds of humanitarian agencies had descended on the population duplicating efforts and yet completely missing the need in other areas. The government was ostensibly trying to coordinate the effort, however the mass chaos was undeniable.

Through the Leupold Ultra M3 fixed power sight, she tracked the movements of Henri LeRoy, leader of this tiny island nation, violator of human rights and dignity, and all around poor excuse for a human being.

Sickness roiled in her stomach. The power bar she'd eaten for breakfast threatened to add to the rubble pile as she tried to figure out how in the hell she'd ended up here. Back behind a sniper rifle with the power over life and death trembling in the muscles of her right trigger finger.

Dammit. When she'd decided to take control of her life and quit the FBI, she hadn't wanted to do this any more.

She'd wanted to be a simple relief worker. She'd wanted to connect with her family, brothers and mother.

But that bitch, fate, had slapped her upside the head and now here she was, where she'd sworn she never wanted to be again. Looking through the scope of a high-powered rifle, with a crystal clear head shot and a murky sense of right and wrong.

With little fanfare, she could blast LeRoy's brain matter all over the silk-covered walls and the antique Louis the XIV scrolled chairs in the receiving room of his ridiculously elegant weekend mansion which, since built properly, had sustained minimal damage. Her muscles twitched with the knowledge and acceptance that with one slow slide of her finger, the despotic, amoral leader would be history.

Jess didn't want to kill him, didn't want to be directly responsible for another death. She didn't want this choice. She'd given up this kind of life. She'd left the FBI after a series of high stress cases to get away from the doubt and guilt that had crippled her. To make her own decisions about right and wrong rather than carry out the commands of her bosses.

But if Henri LeRoy lived, chances were astronomical that many other citizens would die.

And yeah, she'd probably been manipulated into this. Actually no probably about it. Assassination had not been listed as one of her duties when she'd joined Global Humanitarian Relief. Damn her brother anyway.

But now all she could do was lay here in the desecrated remains of the former church and hope that her special skill set wouldn't be needed.

Fortunately, she was secondary backup.

And unless several things went horribly wrong, she would break down her weapon, get back to the relief aid encampment, back to actually helping people, and be out of here without ever firing her rifle.

Then she could hand out seed packets to her heart's content and figure out what she was going to do next. If she'd stay with GHR and her brothers, or go. First, she had to get through the next two hours.

But if something did go wrong...she prayed that if she was called upon, she could make the right decision. Make the shot. Cold zero.

 *0 hours earlier*

"ARE YOUR SHOTS UP TO DATE?"

No hello. Jack Stone, Jess's oldest half-brother and more importantly her new boss, was direct and to the point. And she knew better than to interrupt his train of thought. "Yes." She'd had her round of standard inoculations, Tdap, MMR and Hep A & B, including vaccinations for malaria, tuberculosis, and cholera, a month ago.

"My office. Now."

Jess was finally going to get to go into the field. Her heart rate picked up and anticipation zoomed through her body as she mentally reviewed possibilities. But, with his sense of urgency, there was only one logical destination. She was going to Port-du-Bois in the Caribbean. Finally, she was going to get to do some good. Adrenaline flooded her body like a welcome and familiar drug, the buzz nearly making her light headed.

Jack twirled his finger, indicating she should close the door. "Time is critical"

Keisha Johnson, her least favorite employee and sometimes nemesis at the Global Humanitarian Relief headquarters in Monterey, sat in the other chair. Jess didn't even know why the woman didn't like her but she knew she didn't. And the feeling was mutual. Something about Keisha rubbed her the wrong way. Jess thought she might have a thing for Jack, but since Jack was her brother, she couldn't come up with any reason that Keisha would be threatened by her. After all, Keisha knew that Jack was her brother. Keisha was in her early thirties, with kinky black hair, mocha skin, striking hazel eyes, but more importantly she had a killer brain. And an attitude the size of the Pacific Ocean.

Dressed in faded camo pants and a tight army green t-shirt, her youngest brother Connor leaned against the credenza behind Jack's desk arms crossed over his impressive chest.

Jess's heart sunk a little. She wasn't Connor's favorite person. Never had been. He'd never come out and said it but she knew that he resented her. He'd been the baby of the house until she and her mother had come to live with them when Jess and Connor had been eight. Their relationship had always been a bit strained. But with the chip he had on his shoulder, his relationship with everyone was a bit strained. Although it seemed like lately he'd been making an effort to move beyond it.

Her pleasure dimmed. She'd been hoping her first mission wouldn't involve Connor. But she'd get over it.

The door swung open and her middle brother, Riley, sauntered in looking like James Bond right before he hit the baccarat tables. Smoothly shaven jaw, sharp cheekbones, and eyes the color of Ireland's green grass, Riley could charm the pants off the even the most virulent of man haters. It was a gift. He didn't just charm though, Riley was the consummate protector and he truly loved women. His charm was genuine and heartfelt no matter the woman's age, looks, or disposition.

Jess's spirits lifted. Maybe she'd be going with Riley. Except, based on his beautifully tailored suit and designer tie, he didn't appear ready to hit an earthquake-ravaged country.

Ava Sanchez, Jack's sweet and gorgeous assistant, began to close the door gently. Her gaze swept the room, skipped over Riley and cast a fleeting, longing look at Connor, before carefully averting her attention. *Huh.*

"Now that we're all here," Jack said gruffly. Jack had been her hero since the day she and her mother had moved into their father's mansion on Seventeen Mile Drive and he'd picked her up and given her a welcoming hug and a giant smile. Jess's heart flooded with love for her half-brother, who had convinced her to come work for GHR, overly responsible for taking care of the world or at least his little corner of it. "Let's get started."

Keisha dismissed Jess, and cut her gaze back to her phone before focusing back on their boss.

Jess had spent the last several months learning the ins and outs and logistics of humanitarian aid relief. A far cry from her work as an elite sniper for the FBI, when she'd prepped for targeted killings, a fancy, legally-sanctioned term for assassinations, but she had voluntarily retired from her prior employment.

When Jack had requested that she come work at his

company, she'd thought long and hard about the offer. As a child, she never quite fit in. She came to live with them late. She was a girl to their rough boys. Sometimes she wondered if she were incapable of more meaningful connections. As if her heart was stone cold and unable to warm. Except she loved her mother, she adored her big brothers, Jack and Riley. Hell, she even loved Connor. But she'd still felt like that kid staring in the window longingly.

The same thing occurred at the FBI. She was a woman, plenty of those, but women snipers were still rather rare, and she never quite fit in. So after careful consideration, she made the choice to go after what she wanted.

She was going to connect with her brothers, maybe even Connor. And now she was going to be doing good. Not killing people. And she was thrilled.

If she missed that heady rush of adrenaline, the positives of her new situation outweighed the negatives. The logistics of surveillance, the mental calculations of vantage points, line of sight, and wind velocity, the unknowns of security and extraction, were behind her now. And while she had an occasional niggle of regret because she missed the heart pounding anticipation and rush, she was beyond happy to be helping control chaos, not inciting it.

She wasn't going to lie though. Being in the office, rather than in the field, had been a huge change of pace. She was ready for some action.

"You're going to Port-du-Bois." He tossed pictures across his desk.

Hot damn, she'd been right. Adrenaline fluttered through her blood, lighting her up like a familiar friend. She just knew that helping the people of the disaster-ravaged island would give her the same rush as she'd experienced in her previous law enforcement life. Hopefully.

Port-du-Bois. The tiny Caribbean island nation had been decimated by an earthquake two weeks ago.

GHR had been monitoring the situation there since the disaster occurred.

"What's the plan?" Keisha, already thumbing coded notes into her smart phone, got right to the point. She was an efficient bitch. Jess would give her that.

"You've got four hours before you go wheels up."

Four hours wasn't much time.

But Jess's 'go bag' had been packed since her first week on the job. At a moment's notice, she was ready to go save the world from itself. God, she couldn't wait.

"Cover?" Keisha asked.

Cover? Jess hadn't been with Global Humanitarian Relief long, but why would they need a cover?

Jack shot Keisha a pointed look, then turned to Jess.

"You're a relief grunt, and security detail, which gives you permission to carry under the island military restrictions." Jack addressed Jess, "The situation is unstable enough that I want you armed and ready to protect."

Guns. It wasn't that she minded. Hell she'd spent the first six years of her career shooting weapons regularly.

When she interviewed for this job she had known her weapons experience was a plus. Everyone else in the company, except Ava, was former military. But still it was on the tip of her tongue to resist until her brother spoke as if knowing that her gut reaction was to argue. "We aren't the fucking Red Cross and I refuse to leave my people unprotected."

For a moment, shadows flickered in his stippled hazel gaze before he cut back to Keisha. "You'll be coordinating seed and water purification tablet distribution. The boxed supplies are on shrink-wrapped pallets and already on their way." The slow measured look he gave Keisha seemed to indicate something more weighty.

Jess paused at the silent communication between them, and a frisson of unease overshadowed her excitement. When Jack spoke again, her worries scattered.

"Our primary logistics coordinator will be a temporary guy, Colin Davies."

Connor shot a surprised glance at Jack. "Not one of us?"

Jack had the grace to blush. "It isn't a good idea for any former military Stone brothers to be in Port-du-Bois."

Connor's eyebrows rose and he gave a short nod.

"Colin is meeting you en route." Jack aimed a remote at the television in the corner and turned up the sound. "He's already been briefed."

Temporary guy? Who was Colin Davies? And why hadn't she ever met him? And how did a new guy get in charge over Keisha? However, Keisha didn't look pissed. Surprising.

"Once you get on island, he'll assess the situation and give you orders," Jack said. "And you'll follow."

Keisha was frowning as if she'd like to argue about something.

"Are you sure she's ready?" If it had been anyone but Riley asking, it would have likely gotten Jess's back up, but she knew he didn't doubt her abilities, he just wanted to make sure she would be safe.

"She's ready." Jack aimed another slow measuring look, this time at Jess. The shadows in the swirls of his green and gold eyes, which changed colors depending on his mood, seemed vaguely threatening. Threatening? She was imagining things.

Jack finally said, "We need her."

Both Connor and Riley tensed subtly. Not wanting to jeopardize her opportunity, Jess nodded confidently. But inside she wondered...what had that little flicker been all about? What wasn't he telling her?

4 *2 hours earlier*

THE CHOPPER'S rotor blades swirled, trying to suck her into the updraft, as the Sikorsky SH-3 Sea-King flown by the U.S. Marine Corps lifted up and away. Jess was surprised GHR had been able to use military resources to get them onto this ship but she wasn't about to ask Keisha how GHR made that happen. She'd save that question for her big brother when she got home.

The ship's engines ground beneath her feet with a subtle chug and her stomach let her know she wasn't on land. Beside Jess, Keisha staggered and nearly fell. Not so perfect. As Jess managed to keep her sea legs, a little zing of triumph zipped through her.

Spotlights illuminated the LZ in blinding relief and cast the surrounding deck in darkness. A shadow detached from the murky side of the command tower. The silhouette was male. A little over six feet, lean, graceful, with

something familiar in his movement as he sauntered toward them.

The glow from the landing pad bled over his features as he drew near. And when his face was revealed, her brain processed details. The arch of his brow, the almost aristocratic cheekbones, the sensual lips and windswept light brown hair. She'd barely slept in the last thirty hours which is why her brain didn't make the leap at first. But...she knew this guy.

Intimately.

His name hadn't been Colin when she'd had sex with him. It had been Niles. A stuffy name for a very *not stuffy* guy. Of course, they hadn't exchanged last names so he likely didn't know her last name was Stone. The sex had been smoking hot and a little too intimate for her comfort.

As a result, the last time she'd seen him, she'd been sneaking out of his hotel room at five in the morning, in a very small, very clingy little black dress, shoes dangling from two fingertips, after a particularly stressful op had almost gone totally south. As in *dead* south.

Jess's gaze narrowed in on his face, watching his eyes, difficult in the encroaching darkness. He faltered, so briefly that if she hadn't expressly been watching, she'd have missed it.

Motor oil and sea water mixed in the air as the whup-whup-whup of the helo's blades faded into the distance.

Without acknowledging any recognition, the new guy leaned down and grabbed the two extra duffels she and Keisha had brought. He jerked his head toward the door to the bunking quarters. They had several hours until the ship reached the island. It certainly seemed as if he didn't plan on discussing old times. So that's how this was going to play out.

Fine.

Of course, she looked a little different now. She'd changed her hair color, again. Now she had ribbons of blond and brown and mahogany. When they'd met before she'd had auburn hair. So maybe he really didn't recognize her.

Her heart thumped in anticipation as she realized she was about to be a part of her first humanitarian mission. After years of working for the FBI, furthering the agenda of the U.S. government at the expense of her own morals in ethically gray areas, she was finally going to do something good.

Something worthy.

No killing involved.

Jess followed Niles, er, Colin.

But the niggling doubt that wormed into her consciousness at the exact moment she'd recognized him wouldn't leave her alone. Uncertainty and apprehension rolled through her.

What was he doing here? Did her brother know Colin used to be SAS? That was a stupid thought. Sure he did. She was the only employee who wasn't former military. And she was assuming that Niles...Colin was not still active duty.

They moved quickly to the covered deck area, the grind of the ship's engines loud in the small enclosed space. "I'm Jess." She shoved out her hand and braced for the contact.

"Colin." He nodded without touching her.

"This is my first relief effort." She volunteered the information hoping for more from him. Skills and training kicked in as she assessed him calmly.

"Brilliant," he clipped.

She remembered him using that exact word when he slid inside her for the first time. Jess's gaze shot to his, and for a moment, heat and memory blazed, burning his cool gray gaze hot.

But then the fire extinguished and she was left cold.

She was even colder when she considered his presence on this boat. What were the odds that he too had grown tired of the increasingly complicated ethics of international politics and government machinations and decided to go humanitarian? At the exact time as she had?

Pretty damn slim.

When she'd been pouring out her heart between bouts of sweaty sex, she'd revealed her vulnerability and her uncertainty about her chosen profession. But Niles had done no such thing.

So what did his presence mean?

It was a well known fact that most intelligence agencies sent in operatives during relief efforts in order to get the lay of land of unstable countries. Could that be his angle? But then how did he get hooked up with GHR? And did her brother know?

She had minimal facts about his former occupation. He'd calmly and efficiently defused the bomb in the Tube station when they met previously. He was British. And totally hot in bed. Beyond swooning over his accent while he went down on her, she didn't know any more details about him.

They'd been in the right place at the wrong time and almost gotten themselves blown up, but luckily he'd been able to deactivate the explosives before the threatened deadline.

Jess had been the lookout in the small supply room, rifle trained on the crowd, vigilantly searching for anyone who looked out of place as the British police tried to calmly evacuate the crowded terminal. They'd both known that if something went wrong, they were dead. It had been the most terrifying and the most exciting hours of her life.

After cleaning up and several debrief interviews, including a mission post mortem, they'd both been nearly dead on their feet when they'd randomly met in the elevator of their hotel. Somehow the smoldering looks that had simmered throughout their time locked in a room with a ticking device had turned into a smoking hot encounter in his hotel room.

They'd planned to go to dinner, but when Jess met him in the hallway, clad in her sexy LBD that weighed about one ounce and left lots of room for her rifle and ammunition in her suitcase, they had stumbled into his room and never come out. Dinner had been forgotten in a haze of scorching lust.

Jess certainly couldn't ask any questions about how he'd gotten from that op to this place. Not until they were alone. No way in hell was she exposing herself, or his past, to perfect Keisha.

Besides, Jess had no idea what or if Keisha had security clearance. Proper procedure would be to let it go. Their prior mission didn't have any bearing on this humanitarian one...unless he wasn't former SAS but had in some way insinuated into the GHR ranks in order to carry out a separate, subversive agenda.

She wasn't going to let that happen.

HOLY SHITE. He'd had sex with Jack Stone's little sister.

When Jack had called to ask for a favor, and requested Colin head this op to keep an eye on his little sister, Colin had said yes in a heartbeat.

Thanks to a particularly hairy situation in Iraq a few years ago, he owed Jack his life. If Jack hadn't covered for him, Colin would be six feet under in a miserable desert in an unmarked grave. So when Jack had asked, the answer had been an easy yes. The last few months on the job had been stressful and disheartening. He was getting tired of dealing with the dregs of humanity and defusing their attempts to destroy. It was the perfect time to pay Jack back and Colin needed a break.

Jack had said in his gravelly 'I mean business' voice, "And just so we're clear. Don't touch my sister."

Colin had figured no problem and replied, "Of course not."

He would never in a million years betray his friendship with Jack over a woman. Not to be immodest, but he could get women whenever he wanted, he had no need to tread there. So what if he hadn't had sex in about six months? Ever since he'd hooked up with a smoking hot FBI agent that he couldn't seem to get out of his brain, his fantasies, or his dreams. He had figured keeping his hands off Jack's little sis was a no brainer.

What were the fucking odds that the FBI agent he couldn't get off his mind was also Jack's sister? When they'd met, they hadn't exactly exchanged life histories. Not even last names. Only extreme sexual pleasure for hours on end. And a few vulnerable moments in the dark.

His main objective for this mission had been to keep an eye on Jack's little sis and make sure that the op had no problems so he could relieve his debt to his friend.

But bugger it all, he hadn't been able to forget the way they had combusted in that hotel room. At the time he'd written it off to a serious excess of adrenaline and a case of 'Thank God we're alive, let's have sex' moment."

Seeing her again, he had to admit that was a lie. They had exploded faster than PE4 with a high heat detonator. You got to know a person when your lives were on the line and you could be sharing your last moments on earth with them. She had been über-cool under pressure and still managed to crack a few jokes to relieve the tension.

He had admired her steadiness and calm in the face of possible death. And he'd been attracted to her even before he'd seen her in the hotel elevator. But when she'd arrived for dinner in that excuse for a dress, Colin's lust had taken over his body and roared through him like an out of control Charing Cross train. The sex had been the best, culminating in the most amazing night of his life. He hadn't been able to forget her. Now here she was, right in front of him.

And he couldn't touch her. He'd promised Jack.

CHAPTER 4

*2**0 hours earlier*

SHE HADN'T BEEN able to get close to Colin Davies. When they disembarked from the ship, he had hit the ground at Mach speed, tersely issuing orders. "Stone, get the manifests for the pallets and double check that we have all our shipments. Sometimes things go missing."

Jess had nodded.

He handed her a clipboard and a heavy backpack. The heat of his body seemed to surround her with a suffocating attraction. To which he seemed oblivious, damn him. Colin said softly, "Here are your supplies. Keep them with you at all times."

In training, she'd been warned to keep supplies on her person or they were likely to disappear. And if stuff disappeared, she'd be out of luck. Jess curled her arms through the pack and hefted the weight onto her shoulders. The familiar heaviness of her pack felt suspiciously like the twenty pounds of a Remington M24 SWS with a sound suppressor. Her sniper system of choice. What the hell? It was tempting to look inside right away but since she was deep in the chaos of the relief encampment, she wouldn't check the contents until she was alone.

Since this was her first official job with GHR she needed to follow protocol to the letter, and protocol dictated that she keep the contents of her personal backpack private.

"Johnson, you need to set up a staging area."

Keisha was the logistics person, setting up the trucks, distribution sites, and handling everything from the tents erected for the relief workers in the outlying field of the decimated airport, to coordinating with the local military when the roads were passable so that GHR could get the seed packets and water purification tablets in the hands of the inland villagers that needed them.

He barked out more orders as he split his attention between Jess, Keisha, and the SAT phone practically attached to his ear, and answered just about any question thrown at him. Jess wanted to get him alone for just a few minutes so that she could find out what he was really doing here.

But after twelve hours on the ground, she wondered if she'd ever be able to get him alone. And she really needed to talk to him about her duties. Although GHR served both the needs of the individual and the overall country, so far they hadn't done anything but set up.

For her first time out, Jess was just a worker grunt. She hadn't had time to train for anything else. She was also backup security, in case the local population got a little too restless while waiting in line for their supplies. Sadly it happened.

Colin was mainly supposed to be the second prong, the

money guy, meeting with the small country's leader to facilitate transferring the pledged funds into the country's bank accounts so that the clearing of debris and then rebuilding of the infrastructure could get started. Although, once that was accomplished, he'd be in the thick of things helping distribute supplies as well.

After a really long day and no opportunity to speak to Colin, she had finally opened her pack.

She hated it but she'd been right.

When she'd gone to inspect the contents of her backpack, the elite sniper rifle stared back at her from the shadowed depths of the bag. This was no crowd control weapon and employee defense tool. This weapon was designed for one thing only.

Killing.

A heavy despair settled over her. What had she gotten herself into? And what hadn't her brother told her? She'd like ten minutes alone in a room with Jack right now. The questions were piling up and she had no one to talk to.

She had no choice but seek out Colin Davies and find out just what the hell was going on.

Half an hour later, she approached his tent which served as both his office and his sleeping quarters. The heavy canvas structure was set off to the side, as close to the encroaching woods as it could get without actually being in the trees.

Jess knocked at the flap and then pushed her way inside.

The temperature outside had cooled to a sweltering ninety-five degrees. A battery run camp lantern hung over his workspace, giving off a soft glow and turning the atmosphere in the tent intimate.

Colin sat at his 'desk', a flimsy card table, looking no less dangerous or sexy than he had six months ago after he'd diffused the bomb. However, his attitude now came across as uninterested, even bored. As if he were completely unaffected by her presence, as if he hadn't had his tongue down her throat within hours the first time they'd met.

"What do you need, Stone?" He signed a paper with a flourish and then looked up from the stack of shipping manifests and worn spiral notepad on the desktop.

"I need to talk to you about the contents of my backpack."

"No, you don't." His mouth tightened, his full lips flattening so subtly that she wasn't even sure she'd seen it as he looked at her without actually looking at her. It was a nifty trick.

"Uh, yeah, I really do."

"I'd advise against it." He was concentrating on the sheet in front of him and not giving her concerns the time of day. Since she was trained to notice small details she observed that his fingers stayed loose and firm on the pen he held. He wasn't taking her seriously. And that pissed her off.

"Don't freaking patronize me." Her voice rose.

In a flash he had shoved back the metal folding chair and circled around the flimsy card table. He stood so close she could feel the heat from his body surround her. Like he was a magnetic tractor beam and she was a cross-section steel, sniper rifle receiver, her body gravitated toward him involuntarily. "This is not the time to raise your voice," he said almost soundlessly, his words barely audible in the stifling confines of the dark tent.

God, she really wanted to step back, step away from the blinding attraction that hit her every time she was near him. But she recognized the unspoken words of his body language and she could not afford to show any weakness. She couldn't let him know how much he affected her.

Especially since he seemed completely unaware of her as a woman. So she stayed still, her body far too close to his, and focused on her larger problem. "This is not what I signed up for."

If anything he leaned closer. Her heart thudded in her chest and her nipples beaded at the scent of warm, sweaty male and a slight hint of Taylor's sandalwood and cedar aftershave. "You know your way around the contents, correct?"

He knew the answer. She'd used the same rifle in London last year.

"Why do I have a death stick?" she snapped in a soft voice. The privacy in the relief tent village was nonexistent and she sure didn't want anyone else to hear their discussion about the contents of her bag.

Before she could blink, Colin wrapped his arms around her and cradled her close.

One of the things that struck her in London was the overwhelming physical reaction that hit her when they were in the same room. Her pulse slowed, her blood thudded through her veins, pooled in her groin, and tingled in the tips of her fingers. Oddly, the sensations were similar to her physiological responses when she was getting ready to take a shot.

Adrenaline dumped into her system as he nuzzled the ultra-sensitive spot behind her ear. For anyone observing them through the tent walls, their silhouettes would be highlighted by the lantern and create a completely different impression about what was happening between them. "Not now."

Jess pressed away from his embrace before she lost all reason, fighting the instinct to snake her arms around him and put her tongue in his mouth.

She slung the bag onto the dirt floor at their feet. "When will be a good time?"

When he didn't answer, she eyed the SAT phone on his desk. She really needed to talk to someone about this. If he wouldn't answer, she'd call Jack.

Colin took note of where her gaze was focused. "Not a chance."

Right. She knew that. The odds that satellite communications were being monitored was one hundred percent. "I'm not leaving this tent until I get some answers."

He released her waistband and flexed his hands then curled them into fists, as if trying to resist touching her again. But they were still so close their bodies brushed with each inhale and exhale of breath. The temperature in the small tent ramped up about a thousand degrees. Her nipples tightened and her sex softened.

God, she was trying to resist the siren lure of lust that dumped into her system with the proximity of his mouth. He rubbed his nose along the shell of her ear and his breath puffed erotically against her skin, the actions completely at odds with his next words. "They just confirmed the first deaths from cholera."

She couldn't think. She swayed toward him, and wondered what cholera had to do with the way her blood buzzed and her breath shortened.

Colin stepped back, the loss of his body heat like an ice bath. She swore she had felt his lips against her hair. But in a back to business manner, he pulled out his smart phone, sifted through pictures until he found the one he wanted. Then he held the phone close to her so she could see.

Jess stared at the picture. Henri LeRoy, the president of the small island country, was...taking a bath? Her brain

could not make the connection between the picture and the contents of her backpack.

This was grounds for the Global Humanitarian Relief, and her brother, to give her a sniper rifle?

She blinked, looked up at Colin, trying to ignore the raging attraction that wasn't going away no matter how hard she tried to ignore it. He was practically dead on his feet, the shadows under his eyes should have detracted from his physical presence but instead his body still screamed sex on a stick. She wondered if he'd look that worn out after spending a weekend in bed on six hundred thread count sheets and living off room service.

"That bath water is bottled." His words were so soft she had to lean closer, and was sucked into a vortex of arousal so strong, it took a few seconds for his meaning to sink in.

The country was drowning in sewage. Their infrastructure destroyed. No running water. Tent cities. Starvation. Limited medical supplies and personnel. A shortage of water purification tablets. Clean water tanker trucks couldn't get to outlying areas because the roads needed to be cleared of rubble or were simply so damaged they ceased to exist any more.

And LeRoy was using precious bottled clean water to take a bath?

Colin leaned forward until his mouth was a hairsbreadth away from her ear. "He's dirty." The puff of breath against her neck shivered over her.

He wasn't talking about LeRoy needing a bath.

A sick feeling churned in the pit of her stomach as the lukewarm military MRE spaghetti and meatballs she'd slurped down for dinner churned up acid.

However she took his meaning, she was going to make him say it.

She'd given up that life. She'd given up 'targeted killings', a nice sanitized phrase for what really happened. Assassination.

That's why she'd taken this relief job. To help people.

"But...that's not why I took this job," she replied helplessly. She swayed toward him, as her mind rejected the truth that he was shoving at her, replacing her ideals with a completely different reality.

"You're going to have to take that up with Jack." Colin stepped back. "Your brother," he said forcefully.

She had no idea what prompted the statement. Colin knew Jack was her brother. Why bring that up? "Believe me. I will but—"

Colin crowded into her personal space again. "Up until now, it was believed LeRoy was doing everything possible to speed the recovery from the earthquake," Colin continued softly. He was pressed up against her. His lips brushed hers, even as his hands curled around her waist. To anyone outside the tent, they probably looked like lovers, with his arms curled around her waist and her breasts pressed against his chest. But she could feel the resistance to her body in the the stiff way he held her tight to him yet also seemed to be keeping her away.

They had been lovers. But with every word, her attraction fizzled and deflated. Because, if they were only here to do good work, there would be no need for Colin to have surveillance against the country's leader. And since Jack had specifically told her to follow Colin Davies' instructions, he'd prepared for a worst-case scenario and supplied her with a sniper rifle. A sense of despair at her naivete settled over her.

Before she could wallow more, Colin spoke again, "This

photograph and the damning financial evidence tell a different story.”

“What evidence?” Betrayal burned in her gut.

“Aid money went missing.” Colin said softly, “We’ve had forensic accountants working around the clock to find it.”

“Where?” But the dread in her stomach continue to build. It was going to be bad.

He pulled her toward his desk. Colin sat down abruptly, spread his legs and pulled her into the V of his thighs. Her body snugged up against his, her core and his erection were in perfect alignment. She was so close she could see the striations of gray in his pale eyes. Heat, that had nothing to do with the temperature outside, rose between them.

Colin slapped at a report on top of his desk. “In the LeRoy’s numbered bank account on Turks and Caicos.”

Missing aid. The leader of the country was stealing from the poor, starving, devastated, dying citizens. She pressed her forehead to his, and cupped his jaw. As if his skin was like a touchstone to the truth. She wished she could rewind and change her decision to go to work for for her brother. To ask more questions in the interview process. To maybe investigate the company a little further. Instead of jumping at the chance to get to work for a relief organization and her half brother, and ignoring the little niggle of doubt that crept in when Jack had asked about her sniper experience. Fuck.

But still she grasped at straws. “But GHR is a relief organization.” As if she could insist that’s all they were.

“Quite right.” He regarded her steadily from with his unusual gray eyes. Eyes she’d likened to a cloudless sky when he’d been sliding into her thick, hot, and hard. Jess’s breath stuttered in her chest as she remembered.

“Most of the time,” he finished.

"I didn't sign on for this." She was shaking her head violently. The action revved up the rest of her body. No. No. No. Her head pounded in time to the denial spreading through her. She wanted to scream.

"You're secondary backup." Colin wrapped his arm around her shoulder, dug his fingers into her hair and held her held still, his cheek against hers and his lips pressed up against her ear. In a hard voice, he said, "Just in case."

Jack and Global Humanitarian Relief had to know very well that killing LeRoy outright was a mistake of epic proportions.

Anarchy would reign and they would have a military coup on their hands within hours. The targeted killing of a leader like Henri LeRoy was an extremely delicate matter that usually took months of planning and careful set up of the leader's replacement.

"You can't do this," she whispered fiercely. "The entire country will be thrown into disarray."

"We have no choice," Colin shot back. "And it's already in disarray. Just look around you."

"Who the hell are you to make that decision?"

He ignored her question, ignored her concern. "Doesn't matter who I am," he replied softly. "What matters is who are you going to be?"

Jess made a sound of defeat. She had no answer. She didn't know.

Colin's heart stuttered at the devastation on her face. He remembered her confessions of uncertainty about her job in the heated, private, sheltered coccoon of anonymity from six months ago. She never thought she'd see him again. He never thought he'd see her again. Any revelations they had made should have stayed buried in their memories. But he remembered, and he ached for her now.

The need to comfort her overrode his reluctance. This was a very, very bad idea. On so many levels, and yet he couldn't help himself. "Hey," he murmured. His hands were fisted in the waist of her jeans as he pulled her closer. Her thick cotton tank bared her shoulders and toned arms. Her clunky hiking boots thunked on the dirt floor as she allowed him to comfort her. The boots should not have been sexy, but the moment she'd stepped between his legs, his cock had surged to life. He was freaking practically asleep on his feet but that hadn't mattered to his libido from the moment she'd walked into his tent.

His head was screaming at him, "Jack's sister!" His body was screaming right back, "I don't care!"

There had been a moment on the ship, when he hadn't seen her face yet but as if his body had recognized hers, he'd been zapped by a bolt of attraction. Before he'd even realized his fantasy woman was there. The woman who'd been haunting his dreams for months.

She stood stiffly in his arms, not moving. Her forehead was pressed against his neck, the only other place they touched was her hips against his spread thighs. She should smell awful, and yet her skin glowed and the refreshing scent of lemon and coconut wafted from her body.

Colin had the insane urge to lick the delicate skin of her collarbone and see if she tasted half as good as she smelled.

Jess sighed. Her breath feathered along his chest. And she finally relented. Her slender arms, full of strength, sleek muscles strong enough to keep a sniper rifle steady and fire with a highly effective accuracy rate, yet still feminine, curved around his shoulders.

Finally.

She inhaled sharply. Her breasts pillowed against his chest and her body melted against his. Colin gave in to the urge to touch her. He had suppressed the feeling since she walked into his tent but now he was done resisting.

He pressed an open-mouthed wet kiss against the tender hollow of her neck. Her heartbeat pulsed strong and steady beneath his lips. He sucked gently and was rewarded when she subtly rocked her hips into his erection.

Colin slid his palms up her slightly damp tank top until her breasts rested in his hands. He thumbed the aroused peaks of her nipples through the ribbed cotton and groaned soundlessly as she sighed into his ear.

She sank further into his embrace, her body softening, preparing for him. Six months ago he'd worshipped every inch of her. He'd memorized each sensitive spot that caused her breath to hitch, each touch that ratcheted her arousal and each intense kiss that ramped up her response.

With perfect recall, he skimmed one hand down her taut stomach. He followed his hand and kissed a slow path down the center of her chest, pausing after each kiss to breathe in her scent and gauge where to caress next.

Colin delved beneath the army green tank and slowly slid the material up her torso, and proceeded to eat her up with little sensual nibbles; A swirl of tongue in her bellybutton caused her stomach to contract hard against his mouth. He dropped wet, sucking kisses along each rib and worked his way up to the underside of her perfect breasts. Her bra was a utilitarian nude cotton but Colin merely unhooked the front clasp and cupped her in his hands. Each globe was a perfect handful. Colin ran his tongue along her skin, up and over the curve until he found her flushed raspberry nipple.

With a voracious need, he closed his lips over the puckered nub and sucked her into his mouth.

She arched into his carnal kiss.

Jess was the picture of erotic abandon with her shirt pushed up around her collarbone, her neck arched gracefully, and her multi-hued braid fell down her bowed back. She clutched his head to her breast, and rolled her hips into the hot brand of his erection. But even as her body responded to his with unbridled passion, he could feel her emotional reticence. He hardened even further as she purposely rubbed herself against the pipe in his cargoes.

It had been like this in England too. They'd barely touched each other and her clothes were coming off and he was about two seconds from blowing.

"This is a very bad idea," he said, even as he sipped and kissed his way to her other nipple. God forbid he not give equal attention to both her breasts.

"Mmmm, hmmm," she agreed as she scraped her nails down his back and tugged his t-shirt out of his pants.

He stopped suckling her long enough for her to yank the shirt up his body and over his head. Then he returned his attention to her breasts.

As soon as his chest was bare, Jess stroked her hands over his body, stopping to play with his nipples and then heading south to his waistband. With greedy fingers, she quickly unbuckled his webbed belt, and unzipped his fly.

"Commando," she murmured. "Love that."

A crash from somewhere outside his tent stole Colin's attention momentarily. He held her neck in one hand, with his other hand he continued to play with her breasts, while he carefully searched the shadows for any threat. As he assured himself there was no concern, he realized that anyone outside would have a clear view of what they were doing. "Time to move, love."

The dazed look in her glowing green eyes was a total ego boost. She had abandoned the need to hold back and had relaxed against him. He grinned and lifted her into his arms. Colin carried her to the twin size cot shoved in the back corner of his tent where they would be mostly hidden behind files and the desk. It was darker here but he could still see her tanned skin shimmering with a light sheen of perspiration as he lay her down on the rough cotton sheets. With an impatient jerk, he ripped the tank up and over her head.

Before he could think about what a mistake this was, he maneuvered alongside her on the narrow bed. Colin cupped her head in his palm and held her still for his kiss. The meeting of their mouths was frantic, urgent, as if she couldn't get enough of his taste. He inserted his leg between hers and the heat of her sex seared his thigh. Her arousal, their mingled scents, perfumed the close air of the tent. Her naked breasts rubbed against his pectorals, as they melded together. Her strong deadly hands already had his pants down around his thighs so she could reach his cock. Her supple fingers wrapped around him and Colin's eyes rolled back in his head.

Shite. Her firm grip and the erotic slide of her hand on his cock were heaven. It had been six long months since he'd felt anything but the company of his own hand.

He skimmed his palm down her concave stomach and deftly unbuttoned her jeans. In the sticky humidity getting her pants off was going to be a bitch. He couldn't wait that long to feel her again. Colin pressed the heel of his hand flat against her belly and slid his fingers under the plain elastic band of her cotton panties before he entered her hot wet depths.

With his middle finger he rubbed at the button of her clit feeling the wetness that already coated her curls. He experienced a moment of triumph. When he slid his finger inside, her low throaty moan rippled in the air, and his spirits soared. Fuck, yes.

She gripped him firm and tight in her slightly callused palm and proceeded to rock his world. The ferocity of her kiss took him by surprise. She devoured his mouth, nipped his bottom lip and then thrust her tongue inside to the rhythm of her hand on his cock.

Colin couldn't bear it any longer. He needed to be inside her. Yesterday.

He withdrew his finger, beyond pleased at her involuntary whimper and quickly shoved her jeans down to her knees. Jess planted her feet and lifted her hips to help him rip the jeans down her legs but then she needed to get her shoes off. Colin went to work on his own cargo pants. The Velcro flap ripped open loudly in the still air, the only other sound was their mingled breaths. He slipped the foil packet from one of the patch pockets then dumped the pants on the floor and turned back to her.

Jess's bra dangled from her shoulders. The glimmer of light from the glow of a nearby tent cast shadows over her face, visible were the glint in her hazel eyes, her wet nipples from his mouth, and the rapid rise and fall of her chest as she waited for him to protect her.

He remembered everything about their one intensely erotic encounter in London. With unerring accuracy, he skimmed his palm along the outside of her thigh then gently lifted her leg and curled it over his hip, opening her to his sensual invasion. After donning the condom, in one smooth move, Colin slid his cock inside her slick channel and savored the sensation of coming home.

Jess caught her breath and canted her hips toward him.

Her hands were insistent and hard on his butt as she urged him silently forward. But Colin had no intention of taking this too fast, he was going to savor the hot clasp of her sex.

He began a slow easy glide in and out of her body, angling his hips so that with every movement he rubbed that hidden spot. Each time her body tensed and tightened around him. Colin's balls tightened and his orgasm built at the base of his spine. Even so, he kept his movements deliberate and far too slow for his sweet impatient Jess.

She squeezed his ass and whispered harshly, "Faster."

"All in good time, love." Colin laughed softly at her growl of frustration.

She firmly took matters into her hands and rubbed her index finger along the swollen gland beneath his balls. "Masochist," she taunted, trying to goad him into going faster.

To appease her, he increased his pace and the intensity of his thrusts.

"Ah, love." He groaned again as her sweet channel squeezed harder, and he abandoned his attempts to tease her. She approached sex like she approached life: Head on and insistent, with no apologies for who she is and what she wants. He loved that about her.

Jess writhed in frustration. She wanted to come and she wanted it now. What the hell was with his need to control every little detail? The last time they'd been together she hadn't minded but right now she wanted to screech at him.

She slammed against him, and clenched her hands on his ass so hard, he'd have marks later, she thought with a fierce thrill.

That bundle of nerves inside seemed to swell so that each time he moved inside her the head of his cock massaged her g-spot and ramped her body to a new level.

Jess's focus narrowed to each glide of his body. His sleek

muscles surrounded her. Her hearing tunneled to the chirp of the crickets outside the tent, the swish of wind through the encampment, and the rustle of the sheets as he moved inside her. A tingle started at the tips of her toes and zipped through her body like lightening. Pure silence rent the air, just like those precious seconds before she pulled the trigger.

Every tiny detail was hyper-exaggerated, the ridged head of his cock, the slick slippery wrap of his arms around her, the meaty bulk of his body between her split thighs, the heft of his ass in her hands. For one moment of expectancy, she hung on the precipice.

Then with one powerful thrust, he swelled even harder inside her, and she shot over the edge with the force of a round exiting the rifle's barrel. Her mind and body fragmented into a zillion pieces as she lost sight and sound and could only feel as her sex contracted almost painfully around his hard, thick length.

Jess swallowed a gasp, trying desperately to be silent. Colin powered in and out of her, each pummeling thrust hit her g-spot, forcing her orgasm to go on and on. The need to let loose a keening moan as sensations bombarded her was enormous. Jess sank her teeth into the bunched muscles of his shoulder to hold back the erotic sound as Colin pumped inside her still hard and big. Each throb sent an answering pulse through her sex. She was one giant nerve ending. And Jess knew that he would hold on until he was sure she had wrung every drop of pleasure from her orgasm.

But she wanted him with her. Wanted him to experience the same intense overwhelming, mind blowing explosion that she had. Because when he did, she moved to another plane.

Every time they had sex, she felt another piece of her soul twine with his. They fit together with an ease that usually took years to obtain. His relaxed acceptance of her need to control and be in charge was unprecedented. Of course, then he blatantly overrode her instincts and took control, which caused a fierce battle of will. But they both were grinning while they fought.

Jess had curled her arms around Colin's head, holding him to her breast, as her sex continued to pulse around his cock. Her heart beat so hard, the thud echoed against his cheek, even as his own heart bumped at the same dizzying rate.

Once he was assured of her satisfaction, Colin hurtled into the abyss of sexual oblivion. His vision dimmed as he emptied his mind as well as his body. Her body continued to pulse around him, and he bent and sucked one tight bud into his mouth hard.

She stifled a small scream and her teeth scored his shoulder again as she tumbled into another orgasm, her sex wringing every last drop of come from his body.

They were both breathing hard as if they'd just run a marathon. A sex marathon, he thought cheekily. But it was more than that. He had missed her. He had missed how they seemed to connect so thoroughly, and how they were so completely in tune sexually. Before he could reveal that completely ridiculous fact, he covered her mouth with his.

He couldn't spout crazy talk if he were otherwise occupied.

Colin wrapped his arms around her and grabbed her ass in his hands. He rocked against her as he came down slowly from the unbelievable high of having her in his arms again. He scattered random kisses on her mouth and face unable to stop touching her.

Then he pressed a sweet kiss, totally at odds with the their insane lust, against her lush mouth.

As reality returned, thoughts of all the reasons why this was such a bad idea crowded his head. Jess was having similar thoughts. He could tell by her rapidly stiffening shoulders, and the tense curve of her jaw, that reality was returning to her too.

And she didn't know the half of it.

Blimey. He'd promised her brother he'd stay away from her. But as she made small attempts to disengage from their embrace, Colin held her tight. "Not yet," he whispered and pressed a tender kiss to the curve of her shoulder. He didn't want to let her go.

Shite. He was in serious trouble.

CHAPTER 5

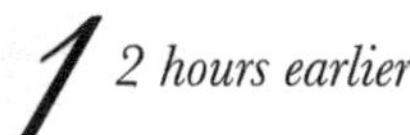

1 *2 hours earlier*

"You certainly didn't waste any time." Keisha cast a snide glance at Jess.

She could barely even focus on the other woman. Her mind was back in that tent, as she went over every single thing that Colin had said to her. She tried to ignore the other memories that crept in. How familiar his hard body felt against hers. How well she fit in the wrap of his arms. How perfect the press of his lips felt against her ear, her mouth, her breasts.

For a few stolen moments, she been enveloped in a sense of completion and an emotional intimacy that she craved. Yet, the idea was insane. She didn't even know him. That surreal sense of fitting together, not just physically but, mentally, couldn't really be possible. Could it? And if it was, what was she going to do about it?

Jess finally realized Keisha was still fuming as she tucked

extra supplies in the nooks and crannies of the back of the truck. "What?"

"Colin." Keisha shoved another box of seed packets into the truck. "Just a word of friendly advice."

There wasn't a bit of friendly in her tone but Jess kept her mouth shut and tried to ignore her. What did she care what Keisha thought? She had bigger problems. However she did have to work with woman. Assuming she stayed at GHR.

"Sure." Even though she had no interest in what Keisha thought.

"At night, with a lantern on, everyone can see everything that happens in that tent."

"I kinda figured." *And I still don't care.* If she chose to have sex with Colin it was no one's business but theirs. And when they were down on the cot, the only way someone could have seen them was if they were specifically watching the shadows.

Keisha's lips tightened. "Just saying you may want to tone down the sexpot skankiness if you want to be taken seriously in this business."

Keisha's criticism didn't necessarily have the desired effect.

In her mind, Jess started to work on expanding her potential cover story, examining angles, filing away information for later, and crafting a fictitious reason that would cover up her real purpose in Port-du-Bois and cover GHR's behind. If people assumed that she was on the island because she was a bed partner for Colin, no one would even think about her in the role of sniper.

At the FBI, she'd been a rarity. A female sniper. One more situation where she didn't quite fit in. But here that could work to GHR's advantage. No one would think Jess, a mere woman and worker grunt, could be a sniper, so if something went wrong and she needed to use her skills against Henri LeRoy, the authorities would likely look for a man.

They would dismiss her presence immediately.

But what about Keisha, was she a straight relief worker or did she have another purpose here? Jesus, Jess had so many questions. She really needed to talk to Jack to get answers, but she couldn't call him. Asking Colin hadn't gone so well. After last night she wasn't about to approach Colin a second time. They'd end up in the sack, having sex again, rather than actually discussing GHR's hidden agenda.

"Thanks." Jess stacked the last crate of seed packets and flipped the truck gate up. She pulled the door shut, and listened for the clunk that indicated the door was secured, so that while they were driving over non-existent roads, the boxes of relief they were set to deliver wouldn't tumble out the back.

Jess swung up into the cab of the truck and set her backpack at her feet. Keisha was already in the driver's seat. The inside of the truck stank of sweaty soldiers and the faint underlying scent of gun oil. She surveyed the interior, cracked vinyl seats, a dashboard that had definitely seen better days, and a GPS system that was useless since most of the roads in the system didn't exist any more. They'd be better off calculating routes based on the position of the sun. But through it all Jess kept her mouth shut.

"You have your pistol?" Keisha pressed in the clutch with her left foot and shifted the stick into first gear.

Jess's stomach churned. "Yes. But shouldn't we be safe?"

Keisha laughed. "In theory, yes. But we've got a trigger happy military and shell-shocked citizens who are desperate for help. These situations are always volatile. And you always need to be prepared."

Keisha was just about to take off when the driver's door swung open. "What the hell?"

"Change of plans," Colin said shortly. "You need to stay here. There's a problem with the special shipment. I'll take the supply run."

Keisha snorted and rolled her eyes. But only Jess saw her expression. "I'll bet."

"We need your expertise," Colin said again. Steadily. Patiently.

Keisha suddenly scrambled to get out of the truck. "Oh. Shit. Okay. Okay. Sorry."

What the heck was that about?

While Keisha scurried off to do whatever thing was keeping her at the relief encampment, Jess shifted in the truck seat. Before she had time to wonder what kind of expertise Keisha had that Colin didn't, or if she really wanted to know, a sharp edge of cracked vinyl scraped her leg and cut her. Jess flinched and tried to ignore the throb in her leg.

She surreptitiously leaned over to look at the cut.

While she was trying to see the damage, Colin leapt into the truck and settled into the driver's seat. Dressed in top of the line hiking boots, tan shorts, and a black fitted t-shirt, his muscled biceps were on display, causing a flutter in her heart. He had wide palms and long fingers with blunt tips. And just remembering his skilled hands as they played over her body sent shivers zipping down her spine. Jess shifted her attention away from his hands. But then her gaze landed on the hairy column of his thighs and she was reminded again of the night they'd spent together in London as she straddled his legs, knees around his slender hips, his fingers tight on her ass as he pounded inside her.

She fanned her face, hoping he wouldn't notice, then prayed if he did, he'd mistake the flush spreading over her skin as a reaction to the heat and not to his proximity.

"What's wrong?"

She should have known he'd pay attention. "Nothing."

"Let me see." Colin leaned toward her. Jess shoved back against the truck door. But it was impossible to avoid his fierce regard. "You're bleeding."

"It's nothing."

"Not here it isn't."

Colin flipped open the glove compartment and pulled out a first aid kit. "With your experience you should know that an open wound in the tropics can be a real problem if it isn't treated properly."

Especially with whatever germs lingered on the ancient truck seat. He was right, dammit. Jess sighed. "Okay. Yes, I think I have a cut."

She twisted her torso to try to see the injury on her upper left hamstring. But the placement of the slice was awkward and she couldn't see a thing.

"Face the window," Colin said tersely.

Jess rolled so that her hip was in the air and extended her left leg.

She heard his swift intake of breath. "What's wrong?"

"Nothing." He pressed a pad with rubbing alcohol on the cut. The sting took her by surprise but she didn't even make a murmur. With gentle strokes, he cleaned the small wound, his movements almost a caress. Then with tender fingers, he smoothed some anti-bacterial Neosporin over the cut.

His actions were oddly arousing. He brushed his fingers

lightly against her skin as he attached the bandage. Jess flushed as her body responded to the soft strokes, remembering the last time he'd had his hands on her thighs. Arousal flooded her.

Jess ignored the gust of awareness that blew through her. What the hell? But she noted how gentle he was with his hands. He'd been like this the last time they'd been together too. As if he knew with absolute certainty how much pressure to use, how hard or soft to touch her, how to caress her to evoke whatever sensation he wanted.

Now it was calming, soothing but before it had been arousing. He'd been able to manipulate her reactions with just the press of his fingers against her skin.

"That should do it." He swirled one last caress against her ultra-sensitive thigh and then removed his hands. She was pretty sure she imagined that his fingers lingered on the back of her leg.

"Let's get going." Jess inwardly cringed at the gruffness of her words.

Colin snapped the first aid kit closed and tossed it back to her. "Fine by me."

Jess put the kit back in the glove box.

She was the one acting weird. She knew it and yet she couldn't seem to turn off her awareness of him. She was the one who couldn't seem to forget the memories of them together. He hadn't mentioned it once. He'd been nothing but professional. This was the perfect time to ask him how he came to be heading the relief effort in Port-du-Bois.

But before she could delve into his reasons for working for Jack, he said, "You need to hide the backpack." Colin gestured to the cracked blue plastic dash. "There's a hidden compartment behind the dash."

"Can't I just put under the seat?"

Colin's intuition was going haywire this morning. It was part of the reason that he'd decided to have Keisha stay in camp. There were rumors that the government had doubled the checkpoints. The relief organizations had been grumbling because the extra security added hours of time and delays in getting aid to the people who needed it the most.

"Humor me," Colin said tersely. Something was off. And he didn't want to be caught unawares by a random patrol or security stop. They couldn't afford to have the rifle discovered. Not only would the military take it, there would be uncomfortable questions about why they had one in the first place.

He turned the key smoothly and listened to the engine rumble for a second before he shifted into reverse. Colin propped his arm on the back of the seat, his hand perilously close to her shoulder. The cab of the truck shrunk by about two hundred percent. Suddenly he was hyper-aware of his fingers so close to her bare skin. But Jess held herself stiff and stubbornly refused to relax against the cracked old vinyl.

He gunned the engine and they shot out of the relief compound at the disabled airport and headed toward their destination.

The air conditioner in the old truck had seen better days. Tepid air chugged out of the vents, minimally cooling the interior of the truck. It was still better than the air from outside, stifling with the heat and dust and decay. The scent was nearly unbearable.

Jess breathed through her nose and thought of a delicate way to begin this conversation. They were confined in the truck with no one to overhear. Then she decided, fuck it. He was the new guy. It seemed an odd coincidence that they both started working for a relief organization at the same time. "How did you end up working for GHR?"

"I owed your brother a favor," Colin said shortly.

Wait, so Colin knew her brother? "Jack?"

His mouth tightened. "Yes."

"How?"

He shifted and arched a brow at her. Finally he answered, "The Spec op community is rather small."

About as specific a non-answer as she was liable to get. "So what's the favor you're doing for him?"

Colin's shoulders tensed and his fingers tightened on the hard plastic steering wheel. "We need to talk about the plan."

Suddenly she couldn't stand the tension in the truck. They weren't going to talk about the plan until they'd discussed what happened in his tent. "What was last night about?" she asked.

He gave her a steamy look. "You have to ask?"

"I find it more than a little suspicious that right after I tell you that I don't want to take out the country's leader you happen to have sex with me."

Colin down shifted the gears as he drove over a particularly bumpy spot in the crumbled road. "Seriously?"

It was suspicious. "You have to admit the timing sucks."

His laugh was a harsh bark. "I don't think you've thought this through princess."

"Don't call me princess."

"It's exactly how you're acting. Like a spoiled princess."

In that moment, Jess could hate him. She had *never* been a spoiled princess. Ever. She was more like Ariel, searching for a world where she belonged. "Fuck you."

"Already did." He shot back. "And I'm going to have the bruises to prove it if your brother finds out."

"My brother?" Jess said incredulously. "Besides being our boss...what does my brother have to do with what happened last night?"

Colin shifted the truck into a lower gear to bobble over the worsening road conditions. At first, Jess thought he was just concentrating on driving.

But after five minutes of silence, she realized he wasn't going to answer.

Screw that. "What. Does. My. Brother. Have. To. Do. With. Last. Night?" she ground out through gritted teeth.

Colin checked the rearview mirror. "We need to discuss the plan."

"You're not going to answer."

"Nope."

"Fine. I'll just ask Jack when I have the chance."

Colin drummed his fingers on the cracked leather seat. "I'd advise against it."

"Okay," Jess said abruptly. But then she considered what he'd implied, bruises. Did he mean her brother would hurt him? That seemed flat out ridiculous. Jack was her half-brother. He was her hero, but he still wouldn't care about her sex life. So she decided to go with his original topic. "Let's talk about the plan."

"About time," he grumbled. "You're secondary backup."

Relief swelled, she wasn't first up to eliminate LeRoy. "So...."

"The plan is to poison him," Colin said softly. "With water."

"Shows a distinct level of irony."

"Yeah."

"So I'm really superfluous?"

"No. You're a world-class sniper, and if we need to take

LeRoy out with lethal force, we need you." His pale gray gaze seemed to skewer her.

But she heard the unspoken caveat, if she refused to target LeRoy, they weren't in a complete bind.

"How's the poison going to be delivered?"

"I'm going to a reception tonight. While the reception is going on, Keisha is going to sneak into the mansion and slip the poison into LeRoy's bath salts."

"How does the poison work?"

"It's slow acting. LeRoy ingest the poison through his skin during his nightly bath. Then he'll go to bed and never wake up."

"What about staff and collateral damage?"

"He has a fetish about being seen naked. When he bathes, he is all alone and drains the tub himself. So everyone else in the mansion should be safe."

"You're sure?"

"Yes."

"So what's my role?"

"If, for some reason, Keisha can't get into the bathroom, I'm going to need you to shoot him." Colin hesitated. "And I need you as backup for Keisha in case she's discovered."

Jess snorted. "You'd think she'd be a little nicer to me then."

"What are you talking about?" Colin frowned.

"Nothing." Jess crossed her arms over her stomach and rubbed her biceps with her palms. "What's the comm situation?"

"I've got wireless earpieces. And voice transmitters that look like buttons. You'll be able to hear everything that's going on."

"What about interception?"

"Code is easy. No names, no specifics, so anyone

listening shouldn't have a clue." Colin flexed his fingers on the wheel. "Our intentions are covert. But you know things go wrong."

Jess asked the question that was bothering her. "So who gets into power with LeRoy gone?"

"Antoine D'Aramitz." Colin released a tight breath as if her question indicated her compliance. "He's a non-denominational religious leader who champions the common people."

"But who decided that he would get power?" Jess demanded angrily. "Our government?"

"Whoa, whoa." Colin slowed down the truck. "Where did that come from?"

"One of the reasons I left the FBI was to get away from playing God," she said bitterly. She'd told her brother that. So why the hell did he send her here?

"Do you really think that LeRoy, a corrupt leader, who is stealing precious resources from his injured, starving, stricken citizens deserves your compassion?"

"Who's to say that whoever replaces him won't be worse?" Jess argued.

Before Colin could answer, they'd arrived at the distribution site.

THEY'D SPENT the day handing out seed packets and water purification tablets. The people had been so grateful for the small bags of seeds that Jess felt guilty about the warm MRE of beef stew she'd gulped down. And she only sipped at her water after watching a mother who gave her kids a drink first, even though it was clear from her split and cracked lips that she was terribly dehydrated.

Throughout the day, she had been by turns amazed and awestruck at Colin's ability to put people at ease.

Jess had been a little uncomfortable. The life of sniper demanded that she was more of an observer rather than someone who interacted with people. She'd perfected that role over the years. The outsider looking in. It had begun at age eight when she and her mother went to live in her father's house with his existing family and continued through her time in the FBI as a female sniper in a male-dominated field.

So six months ago, she'd made the decision to live her life differently. To be engaged. To be present. She'd known going in that adapting to this new life would take her out of her comfort zone. She relished the idea. But old habits were hard to break and she found herself watching rather than participating. But because she was constantly watching, she noticed details that others overlooked.

She'd seen Colin's conspiratorial smile with the tiny boy who had hidden in his mother's skirt. Colin's gentle hug for the woman whose husband had perished. Colin's grave sympathy and compassion for the grandmother whose daughter was missing. He'd treated the men who stood in line with dignity and gave them the respect the deserved for taking care of their family, without the pity that Jess saw reflected on many of the other workers' faces. He calmed the fears of the children when the aftershock hit.

And then Colin had stepped in front of her when the crowd waiting for their supplies got a little unruly. Jess had been bemused by the fact that *he* was trying to protect *her*. She was the one with the pistol and he'd still shielded her from the crowd and herded her back toward the cab of their truck in case they needed to hop inside to shelter from the crush.

After a full day of handing out supplies, the constant battle between smiles so hard her cheeks hurt and an innate need to release her sorrow with tears had taken a toll. She was exhausted.

Because of the mini-riot, they were behind on their schedule.

"We need to get back before the curfew," Colin said. They hopped in their truck and headed back to the main seaside town.

The sun was low in the twilight sky, bright yellow at its center bleeding to a deep red on the edges. The sky rippled with waves of blue, purple, and pink, the colors spectacular from the pollution of the quake. Beauty from destruction.

As they rounded a bend in the makeshift road, they almost ran into the truck in front of them which had come to a full stop. A line of relief aid trucks snaked through the debris field. "Checkpoint," Colin said unnecessarily.

"What time is the reception?" Jess unsnapped her holster and fingered the pistol as she watched the soldiers interrogate the workers two trucks in front of them.

"Keep your mouth shut and don't argue with anything they say," Colin commanded.

"What do you mean?"

A soldier, who was more boy than man, tapped his rifle on Colin's window. "Purpose," he asked in a sing-songy lilting, almost lyrical, voice. His skin was the color of a mahogany wood bowl polished to a brilliant shine that her mother had purchased years ago when they'd been on vacation. Her mother loved that bowl and it was a permanent decoration on their kitchen table.

"We delivered seed packets and water purification tablets," Colin replied evenly.

"Tablets?" The soldier raised his eyebrows and the

whites of his eyes were ultra-bright in the deep brown of his gaunt face. "They all gone?"

"Just about."

"Show me."

Colin got out of the truck cautiously and walked around to the back. He lifted the gate that had covered the transportable boxes of seed bags and the packets of water purification tablets which were like gold in a country with a nearly destroyed infrastructure. The back was mostly empty, and held only the detritus from the packaging, crumpled shrink wrap and flattened boxes.

"How about a little something for me family?"

Colin reached into a pocket on his shorts and handed several seed packets and tablets to the soldier.

As Jess sat tight in the cab of the truck, an unsettling tension gripped her stomach. Colin seemed fine as he joked with the soldier. But somehow she knew that he was concerned. And the fact that she could intuit that he was concerned was a whole other issue. She was completely in tune with him.

Which was kind of freaking her out. She didn't get in tune with people. If anything, she was mostly out of tune. She never quite fit.

Except she'd felt an undeniable connection with him since London. A preternatural communion that defied logic. She could sense his edginess, even though his smile was loose and easy as he closed the truck bed and sauntered loose-hipped and casual back to the driver's side of the truck.

The soldier opened Jess's door and gestured for her to get out. She could practically feel the tension vibrating off Colin but his smile was relaxed and his hands were draped casually over the steering wheel as if he didn't have a care in the world. The young soldier dug through the glove box and peered under the seat.

She was glad she had listened to Colin and hid the Remington in the compartment in the dash. Otherwise she had a feeling that it would now be the property of the Port-du-Bois military. Or at the very least, the soldier in front of her. Jess tensed as he came close to the hidden compartment, but he seemed to miss the seam in the faded plastic dash. And finally he gestured for her to get back in.

The soldier waved them through.

Colin was silent.

She finally couldn't stand it anymore. "What's wrong?"

He tilted his head and cocked a perfectly-sculpted pale brown eyebrow. She was amazed at how well-groomed he appeared. She knew he hadn't had a real shower in two or three days, only cleaning off with baby wipes. And the heat during the day was not conducive to staying cool or clean. Not to mention sleeping in canvas tents on cots barely a foot off the dirt and debris strewn ground made for a very dusty rest.

"What makes you think something's wrong?" he asked.

She wasn't about to admit that she felt connected to him. "Just answer."

"The checkpoint going back *into* the city is unusual."

"How so?"

"If the government is worried about intelligence gathering visitors, the checks are conducted in the morning as the relief trucks are going into the distribution area. Not after everything has been handed out." He glanced into the rearview mirror and frowned. "It's almost as if they are looking for someone. Or something."

"Do you think they somehow got wind of what you, we, have planned?"

Colin drummed his fingers on the steering wheel and shot another look in the rearview mirror. "I hope not."

They drove back toward the coastal city, the interior silent as Jess contemplated the implications of the sentry.

Twilight gently bathed the woods on their right in a soft, romantic light. Driving along the pretty scenery, it would be easy to forget that the entire island was in complete disarray. Jess propped her chin on her fist and gazed out the window appreciating the beauty.

"What are you doing?"

"Thinking about how pretty the sky is."

Colin glanced over at Jess. What the hell was it about her?

All day he'd been distracted by little things. The way she found the beauty in an ugly situation. The curve of her smile as she'd handed out seed packets. Her pert breasts when she'd arched her back looking for relief from standing most of the day. Remembering the sweet wet heat of her as he'd slid home last night. The greedy pull of their attraction was nearly incandescent. The compulsion to find a secluded place and press up against her until no space existed between their bodies was strong. The urge to hold her tight in his arms and refuse to let her go. A thousand times today he'd found himself staring at her and thinking thoughts that were not going to endear him to her brother.

Shite. Those thoughts were going to lose him a friend.

He'd been doing this job as a favor to Jack but after the last few days, Colin realized he liked this work. Sure he was compiling a report that detailed information that could be sold to the both his government and the U.S. but primarily he was engaged in helping people. And he had gotten a surprising thrill from the good deeds of the last few days.

As they rounded the bend in the mostly decimated road,

Colin jammed the brakes on, and the truck slid to a complete stop. "Shite," he muttered.

Jess straightened in her seat.

"Another checkpoint," Colin said. This was not good. And this close to both curfew and the city limits, the inspection of their truck was going to be a lot more thorough. Colin needed to get ready for the reception at the President's mansion. "We need to distract them."

Jess didn't hesitate. "How?"

Colin assessed the soldiers at this checkpoint. More attentive, more intense than the last guy who only wanted a few seed packets for his family. These guys meant business. He and Jess needed to be as non-threatening as possible. "Unbuckle and slide over."

Jess scooted next to him but left a few inches between their bodies.

"You need to plaster yourself to my side." Colin slung his arm around her shoulder, and yanked her snug against his body. His hand dangled above her breast.

With disconcerting predictability, his cock sat up and took notice. "How good an actress are you?"

Her breath caught and Colin couldn't help notice when the side of her breast brushed his chest. Shite. Maybe this was a bad idea.

"Pretty good." She nuzzled behind his ear. "I'll make it work. Don't worry."

Colin kept his left hand on the wheel and with his right arm he pulled her closer. While they were stopped behind another truck, he pressed his nose into her thick braid. She smelled of lemons and freshness. How did she do that? Bathing consisted of baby wipes, unless someone was crazy enough to go in the ocean. The amount of debris on the

shore right now was insane which likely meant that bathing in the ocean would lead to disease or infection.

Colin didn't want touch her. Actually that was the exact opposite of the truth. He wanted to touch her so badly he ached with it. Based on the tension in her body, she felt the same. Colin had figured out from experience that if he put his hands on her, he'd go up in flames. And right now they really couldn't afford the distraction.

Colin had adeptly been ignoring their attraction when she had been all the way across the bench seat leaning on the door. But the warmth from her body suddenly heated him up as she pretended to melt against him, and raised his awareness to an excruciating level. His heart thudded in his chest, and overtook his awareness of their surroundings and bang, banging until he realized that someone was tapping on the window.

"Out of the car, mon."

Colin started and blinked down at the young soldier. He murmured to Jess, "Slide out of the cab on my side after me."

"'Kay."

Thank God she was savvy enough to obey orders when it mattered.

Colin pushed open the truck's door, wincing at the squeal of metal hinges. "What were ya doin' inland?" The guard held the AK 47 loosely in his hand, strap strung around his neck in what appeared to be a casual manner, but Colin knew that with one quick jerk, he could have the weapon locked, loaded and firing.

"We delivered seed packets and water purification tablets," Colin said calmly.

"We want to see da inside."

"Sure thing." Colin feigned a casualness he definitely didn't feel. "Go ahead."

He held Jess's hand and as she exited the truck, then he casually twirled so that his back rested against the truck bed, hips canted out while Jess draped over his relaxed body. She figured out exactly what he wanted and wrapped her arms loosely around his waist, and burrowed into the curve of his neck, so that she was mostly only visible from the back, her face hidden by his arms and shoulders.

The soldier leered at Colin's hand on Jess's nicely rounded ass, which was exactly what Colin wanted, to divert the guy's attention from her face.

The military commander shouted and the harder, older soldier lost his grin and crawled into the cab of the truck. Colin ran his hands up and down Jess's back and prayed that the more experienced soldier didn't find the panel in the dash that hid the backpack with the sniper rifle.

Two more soldiers joined the search, one popped the hood over the engine and peered inside. The other opened the gate in the back of the truck.

Colin slid one hand into Jess's back pocket, the move smooth and familiar. She nipped at his earlobe in warning.

"You smell so good, babe." Colin pretended to ignore the soldiers and kept a running conversation with Jess. The position of their bodies inflamed him like gasoline on a sputtering fire. "How is that possible?"

He really did want to know.

He was sweating as he waited for the shout of the soldiers to indicate they'd found the backpack. His worry hadn't affected his erection though. His body was locked and loaded and ready to fire. Jess didn't say a word at the rod poking her in the stomach. But in retaliation she brushed her breasts against his chest. He should have his entire attention on the soldiers, but the hard points of her nipples diverted him again, splitting his focus between her effect on his body and the search going on beyond them.

"You're distracted by other things." She laughed huskily. "Pretty sure I stink."

She should and yet, she didn't.

"You are driving me crazy," he growled truthfully against her neck.

"Back at 'ya," she quipped back quickly but the simple duck of her chin and the squeeze of her arms around his neck told him she was telling the truth, feeling their strange and overwhelming attraction as well.

He opened his mouth and gave in to the wholly unexpected need to affirm she felt the same. But before he could speak, the soldier in front dropped the hood of the truck back into place and at the exact same time the soldier in the back pulled the door back down. Jess jumped at the noise and planted her head in his shoulder as if embarrassed.

"You're free to go."

And the intimate moment was gone.

 *ow*

JESS HUDDLED in the debris of a church two blocks over from the President's mansion, and through the rifle scope, tracked both Colin and Keisha.

Colin was inside the mansion. He sat in a delicate brocade chair with his legs crossed and a bone china teacup cradled in his oddly delicate grasp. She shivered at the contrast between his rough fingers and the tiny cup as she recalled his dexterity with his hands.

Oil paintings adorned the walls, high ceilings dripped with ornate mouldings, Persian rugs covered the endangered wood floors. Maids poured tea from bone china pots and served tea sandwiches on etched, sterling silver platters.

About twenty men of varying ages mingled in the ornately furnished room. Not a single guest was a woman. The wait staff, all women, were dressed in formal maid uniforms with starched black skirts, a white apron pinafore, and a white peter pan collar.

"Misogynist," Jess mumbled.

The plan was to poison LeRoy. No scent, no discernible traces for an autopsy, unless you were specifically looking for the drug, and slow acting enough that Colin and the other relief organization attendees of this little soiree would be long gone when LeRoy died in his sleep.

Keisha who was supposed to deliver the killing salts to the mansion had been trapped in another section of the city. A mob of citizens grew angry when the distributors of first aid kits ran out and so she was late to the servants' entrance at the back of the mansion.

Keisha had lost her comm device. She'd managed to let them know before the tiny transmitter got ripped from her shirt while she protected the poison. However Keisha could still hear Jess and Colin.

But now Jess tracked Keisha to the back door where she was trying, unsuccessfully it appeared to Jess, to get in. Of course, Jess couldn't hear her so she wasn't completely positive. Jess gave Colin a quick update.

Jess followed Keisha's movements. This was the one part of the plan that Jess had felt was tentative but Keisha had assured both Jess and Colin that she would be able to speak the magic words. Whatever they might be. She hadn't shared. Damn, three days in her company, and Jess wasn't any more thrilled with her than she had been in Monterey.

"Two turned away," Jess updated him softly.

Even as the cook at the back door refused Keisha entrance, a group of women dressed in very short dresses, flat sandals, big party hair and bright red lipstick crowded in the doorway.

"Are my eyes deceiving me or did this asshole get

hookers for his party?" Jess snarled in disgust. "Holy crap, he did."

Her fingers were slick on the stock of the Remington as she contemplated options. Her objections to shooting him had shortened as she lay in the rubble, and the heat seared her skin through her clothes.

Jess observed the reception of the the relief organization officials in LeRoy's mansion. The tiny tea sandwiches made her stomach roil. The people of this country were starving. *Starving*. And he was serving sandwiches made with bread with the edges cut off? Where were those remnants?

"You should go for it," Keisha said angrily.

She had to make a decision.

Did she shoot LeRoy? Keisha had told her to take the shot. They had no other choice. But that wasn't exactly true. Jess thought about the poison that Keisha had. Now that she'd tried to get in and failed, Keisha was off the table. But no one had seen Jess.

If she took the shot, chaos would reign.

She thought about what her brother had said when he'd convinced her to take this job. He'd spoken passionately about their ability to make a difference in the world. There had been a moment when he'd gotten a far away look in his eyes, and murmured about how differences weren't always in the expected manner.

She slowed her breath and her heart rate, listened to the steady thud, getting into her Zen space, as her focus narrowed to the Medal for Humanitarian Relief pinned proudly to LeRoy's chest. An obscene and deceitful display of qualities he didn't possess. A false front he presented to the world.

LeRoy laughed heartily at some comment that Colin had made. With the high-powered lens she observed the

slight tightening round Colin's eyes. He was wondering when the hell he could leave. The signal for him to take off was after Keisha delivered the poison.

With deliberation, she counted her heartbeats, waiting, waiting, for the moment when she could squeeze the trigger and end his life. Jess knew if she killed LeRoy with her sniper rifle the country would be thrown into disarray.

The immediate chaos would throw the already disintegrating social situation into total anarchy. The military would be trying to keep peace rather than distributing the goods and the desperately needed supplies to the citizens.

Jess thought of the young children she'd handed seed packets to this morning. Their gaunt filthy faces as they looked to the packet, one very small pouch between them and total starvation. The grief and shadows in the faces of the people she'd helped today. Their gratitude submerged under the sheer weight of staying alive and staying healthy.

Her chest tightened, restricted by doubt. How could she pull resources away from the very needy?

She looked through the scope again. LeRoy smiled, his teeth white and polished in a shiny clean face. The polar opposite of the dirty, bedraggled people she'd served earlier this afternoon. If she killed him now, the immediate threat would be eliminated but the long term effects to the population would still be there and even more uncertain.

She hadn't asked the right questions earlier when she'd spoken to Colin. She should have asked more about LeRoy's successor. Sure he was a religious leader. But was he a zealot? Did he serve everyone or give special preference to certain religions?

Right now D'Aramitz was the probably the best choice. But who would they chose to take over for him?

Jess didn't know the answers but she did know that the people had no hope with LeRoy in power. A flicker of movement caught Jess's eye as Keisha walked around toward the main street and suddenly she realized there was another way.

And she knew what she had to do. "Two, meet three at the zero site."

She had told both Colin and Keisha where she planned to set up. She was two streets over from the mansion. Keisha acknowledged Jess's order with a nod of her head. Jess had the means to carry out the mission as they'd originally planned, only the execution would be slightly different.

She stared at the mansion, calculating how she could get the poison to LeRoy's bath. Jess was only supposed to provide protection for both Colin and Keisha and in the event that that their plan failed she was supposed to shoot LeRoy and then get back to the tent compound ASAP.

But now that Keisha had bombed, Jess could get the poison in.

"Three will fill in for two."

Colin smiled faintly as if amused at his companion's joke. Then he turned his head so that it seemed almost as if he was staring straight at her. His light gray eyes glittered with heightened intensity and annoyance as he shook his head slightly.

"I am a party girl." Jess tried to get her meaning across without actually explaining. They hadn't come up with code for 'Keisha couldn't get in and now I'm going to take her place'.

The plan was crazy. She was crazy. Adrenaline coursed through her. The natural high a familiar and welcome fizz in her bloodstream. Dammit. She'd missed this. The edge.

The excitement. Even the element of danger felt like coming home.

What the hell did that say about her?

With calm deliberation, Jess began disassembling her sniper rifle. Her hands trembled as she placed the weapon's pieces in the specially fitted backpack and then calmly pulled out the LBD she hadn't worn since the night she'd hooked up with Colin.

Night was almost completely upon the city. She needed to get going.

She managed to shimmy out of her relief worker clothes and into the little dress. Then she swiped blusher on her cheeks and a layer of shiny gloss on her mouth. The little thong flats would have to do since she didn't have any heels.

Her backpack lay next to her. For a moment, Jess wondered at her instincts. Now the reason she'd felt compelled to shove a black knit jersey dress that took minimal space—the same dress she'd worn the night she'd hooked up with Colin six months ago—and the small bag of cosmetics in her backpack, just in case, seemed like serendipity. When she'd been in the FBI it had been standard operating procedure to be ready to change her appearance with a few quick moves and the habit had stuck.

Unfortunately she'd have to take her transmitter off, but she still had her earpiece in. Fortunately Colin couldn't yell at her since he was otherwise occupied.

Jess slid quietly down the debris pile and met Keisha at the base of what used to be the courtyard of the church. They quickly exchanged burdens, Keisha took Jess's backpack and Jess took the poison and taped it to the inside of her thigh.

Keisha gave her head a gentle pat. "Good luck...and thanks."

Jess headed for the back door of the mansion. She knocked on the back door authoritatively. When the cook opened the door, she shoved in, chattering away. "Oh goodness, thanks, I'm so sorry I'm late, can you tell me where I'm supposed go?" she beamed at the rotund cook. She was a large woman with a head full of cornrows and a bemused frown.

She opened her mouth as if to tell Jess to get out.

"I know, I know. I'm late. I got stuck at the security checkpoint." She pointed down at her feet then leaned in and whispered in the cook's ear. "They took my damn shoes. But luckily I had a friend close by who totally wears my size and I could borrow her shoes and then I practically ran all the way here."

The cook still hadn't said a word.

"Please, please let me in." She put her hands together in the prayer position, index fingers to her lips, as she begged. "I need the money." Jess let a little bit of sob trickle through her voice.

Finally, the cook pulled her into the kitchen and shut the door behind Jess. She looked Jess up and down and whispered. "Be careful, milady."

A shiver ran over Jess's spine as she realized that the cook knew something was up. And she was letting her in anyway. She grabbed the woman's hand, and said fervently, "Thank you so much."

"Kat-a-rine." A burly security guard stomped into the kitchen. "What'choo doing?"

"She's with the others."

But the guard had already caught on to Jess's purpose and he smiled slyly. "You're late, missy."

"I-I know," Jess stammered to make it look good but inside she was rolling her eyes. "I had a shoe emergency."

She hoped the silly statement would take him off guard. Instead he gave her a lecherous look. "What you gonna do to make it worth my while to let you in?"

Jess gulped. This situation hadn't been covered in the GHR employee handbook. Shit. She widened her eyes and glanced at his crotch. "Do I have time? I don't want President LeRoy to be mad at you. I thought the guests had already arrived," she said in a breathy voice, reminding the asshole that his boss would be less than happy if she were any later.

The guard peered over his shoulder. "No time now. After the party."

Sure, pal. Jess breathed a mental sigh of relief. One awkward situation down, who knew what?, next.

"Follow me," he grumbled.

"Is there a place where I can freshen up?" she smiled beguilingly at the guard. If she could just get into LeRoy's bathroom, she could unload the poison in the bath salts and get the heck out.

"No." The guard shook his head emphatically. "Guests only."

Dammit. That would have been too easy. Guess this would have to be done the hard way. Hopefully she could figure what the hard way was before she was picked up for the night.

Jess sashayed behind the guard through a massive wide hallway with hand-tied silk Persian rugs and gilded gold-framed portraits of former leaders. Crystal chandeliers hung from high arched ceilings and cast light on a door almost hidden by fancy moulding work. The guard whispered, "You can sneak in this way and no one will notice."

"Thanks," she smiled sultrily and tried to impart every drop of sensuality into the gesture. "See you later, doll."

His teeth were almost blindingly white in his dark face as he shoved her into the room. Jess nearly stumbled, but true to his word, she'd been thrust into the room in a back corner. The other guests were gathered around the buffet table set up at the other end of the large drawing room and no one noticed her less than elegant entrance.

The entire room reeked with the scent of lilies. Jess wondered where in the hell LeRoy had gotten lilies as a decoration?

And then she stopped, caught by an intense, severe stare.

CHAPTER 7

He was going to kill her.

Assuming she made it out of the extremely dangerous situation she'd just willingly put herself into, her life would be forfeit because Colin was going to strangle her.

And then once he got back to the states for the debrief, Jack was going to kill him.

One big happy death circle.

What. The. Fuck?

She had gone completely against plan. This wasn't even plan D, this was plan WTF.

She had on the dress that she'd worn the night that they'd hooked up and even with slightly dirty feet and very little make up on, she was flat out gorgeous.

Colin couldn't take his eyes off her. Neither could half the men in this room. And what the hell did it say about him that he was beyond turned on?

"Ah, I can tell that you see something you like, mon ami," LeRoy teased Colin. If he hadn't been freaked before, he was now in the stratosphere of completely jacked up. Colin didn't want LeRoy anywhere near Jess.

Colin stretched his fingers to forcibly keep his hands from clenching into fists. He couldn't afford to display any kind of weakness. "She is...attractive." *Never show how much you want something.*

This entire plan was a cluster. Keisha had been stopped, Jess had put away her rifle, which he really hadn't wanted to use her anyway. She'd been right. An outright assassination of LeRoy would throw the country into civil unrest. While a natural death would create some difficulties it was nothing compared to what would happen if LeRoy died violently.

LeRoy let out a deep belly laugh, his face wreathed in wrinkles of a smile, his shoulders shook with mirth. He looked like a big fat black Santa and his bowl full of jelly. "I think more than just attractive. My madam has outdone herself." LeRoy slapped him on the shoulder so hard, Colin nearly bent in half. "Avail yourself."

Yeah, cause that would be good for you....wouldn't it you big fat fuck?

Colin was pretty sure there were cameras in the rooms that the guests and their paid 'companions' were encouraged to use.

But he'd made such a big deal of staring at her that now Colin had to pick Jess up for the night. Of course, better him than someone else.

Colin prowled toward Jess, staying to the outside edge of the room so he could continue to observe the occupants. He noted how she moved around the room, mingling with the other guests and managing to keep a fairly even distance between them. Finally Colin had had enough. LeRoy was going to remember that Colin had the hots for a girl he didn't recognize. And hopefully LeRoy would be dead before he could thank the madam for a woman she didn't send.

If Jess wasn't fucking careful she was going to find herself trapped for the night with one of these immoral 'philanthropists' who were willing to use a country's prostitutes even as they proclaimed their philanthropic goal was to aid the poor, disaster-ravaged citizens. It certainly wasn't his job to police them, but he really hoped that Antoine D'Aramitz truly was a man of the cloth and not a secret pervert.

Finally, Colin lost patience with her delay tactics. He stalked straight through the crowd. Jess, who was still keeping the periphery in her vision, didn't realized he'd changed his trajectory. By the time she figured out he was no longer on the edges, it was too late.

Colin stood in front of her and the man she was currently chatting with.

"Bonjour," she said with a sultry smile. Only Colin noticed the nerves beneath her welcoming exterior as she comprehended that he was not happy. Colin nodded to the portly man who was practically salivating at the way her plump breasts spilled out of the low cut top. She'd spread some sort of shimmery powder on the mounds and they glittered in the bright lights of the large room.

"Sorry, old chap. But I do believe she's taken." He curled his fingers around her bare bicep and crowded her body with his. Then he leaned in and whispered in her ear, loud enough for the other man to hear. "I want you."

"Monsieur." She giggled and batted her eyelashes flirtatiously. "How delightfully forward of you."

"I'll make it very worth your while."

The other guy, wide-eyed and mouth hanging open, looked like he might object and challenge Colin for the opportunity to spend some alone time with Jess. So before he could even formally throw his hat in the ring, Colin began to herd Jess toward the exit. He curled his arm around her torso, from the outside the embrace should look lover-like, but hopefully Jess realized that the only way to break his hold would require a serious chop to the solar plexus.

He shouldn't have worried. Jess twined her arm through his and swung her hips languidly as they sauntered toward the door that lead to the guest rooms. Ostensibly the rooms were ready for freshening up, but in reality they were for illicit sexual liaisons with the women that LeRoy provided.

Heat rose from her skin, and her fresh lemon scent and underlying perfume filled his senses. His body responded like she was standing there buck naked. "I am so tempted to put you over my knees and spank you."

She laughed huskily and leaned over to whisper in his ear, "I'd like to see you try."

"Don't push me," he growled.

Jess played the coquette and tilted her head, blonde and brown streaked hair tumbled sexily over one mostly bare shoulder, and over her breast. Her green eyes glittered with some emotion he couldn't quite pin down. Indignation? Frustration? "Don't underestimate me."

Colin found one of the rooms for the guests to 'freshen up' in. He knocked lightly and when no one answered, he shoved the door open. Before she could lay into him, he curled his arm around her shoulders, and pressed her up against the wall covered in delicate, seashell pink silk wallpaper. He rocked his hips into her body, and reveled at the catch in her breath. Very quietly, he whispered in her ear, "Likely bugged, and/or recorded."

Her body stiffened. But as if she immediately realized she had to be on guard, she went liquid.

Yes, she'd caught his meaning. They were likely going to be taped.

And they were going to have to perform, at least to some extent. They had to make it look and sound good before they could wander out, get lost, and hopefully get into LeRoy's bathroom, plant the poison and get out of the mansion before anyone caught them where they shouldn't be.

Getting right on board, Jess dragged her foot up his calf, even as her hands headed south and grabbed his butt. The move tilted her hips into his burgeoning erection. The blood in his body rushed to his cock even as he cupped her breasts through the snug, stretchy black fabric.

Suddenly he was back in that hotel hallway in London.

She was rubbing her body along his and his brain was short circuiting, sending pulses of lust straight to his dick. They needed to be strategizing, and all he could think about was getting inside her. As if he'd die if they weren't connected in the most intimate manner possible in the next five seconds.

Colin scraped his fingers up her bare silky thigh and under her short tight skirt.

As he encountered mostly naked curves, his eyes rolled back in his head. "Fuck me, do you have anything on beneath this?" he snarled. His brain completely shut down.

She laughed. "Thong, monsieur."

Thank fuck, she was staying in character because Colin had completely forgotten that they were players in a dangerous game. Where the hell was his head?

"I'm going to rip it off." He yanked the lace from her body and plunged two fingers inside her. "I'll buy you a new one." He panted.

Jess laughed nervously. "Not necessary, mais merci."

And then she moaned as he trilled his thumb over her clit and a fierce triumph roared through him.

She tried frantically to undo his belt, and clawed at his zipper, scrabbling to get his pants down.

She shoved his underwear to his thighs and squeezed his bare ass. Colin wondered where the cameras were placed and hoped that what they were doing would be mostly hidden by his body. They were going to have to go through with this. If someone were actually listening or watching real time, it would be too suspicious if they didn't now.

Fuck. He wanted to take his time. Spend hours, days, exploring her body, finding all those perfect spots and secret places that sent her into the stratosphere. On crisp sheets with an ocean breeze swirling around them and a bucket of chilled champagne sweating by the bedside. Instead, he was about to fuck her up against a wall.

Colin pulled his fingers from her body and curled his hands underneath her thighs and lifted her up. "Condom in my back pocket."

She pulled the condom out and ripped the package open with her teeth. Jess had a huge grin on her face and her eyes were bright with laughter and desire. And fuck, but that turned him on even more. She was having fun. And she didn't give a damn that there were likely cameras on them.

"Put it on," he gutted out. He was so hard right now, they didn't need the poison, he could club LeRoy to death with his cock.

The touch of her fingers on his cock as she rolled the condom down sent licks of fire through his blood. Jesus, she affected him. Her body told the same story, the feeling was mutual. His fingers were slick from her wet channel and her nipples stabbed his chest. Her breasts were flushed with arousal. And she probably didn't even realize that she

swayed back and forth in tiny hip rocks against his abs, rubbing against him sensuously.

Finally the condom was all the way on. "Brace yourself."

Colin's head went light as all the blood in his body rushed to his groin. In one desperate move, he thrust up into her and at the same time pulled her hips down so he was buried to the hilt. Jess shoved her head back against the wall, the crack echoed in the room. She clutched his shoulders with greedy fingers and a keening moan erupted from her throat as she came from that one powerful invasion.

Her body milked him, her hips rocked almost frantically. Colin powered in and out of her, caught in his own rush of lust. It only took one, two, three thrusts and his orgasm shuddered through him like a powerful shock.

She was wrapped around him like a freaking octopus, as the crazy force of his orgasm practically blew the top of his head off. He might have felt like a total loser for being so quick on the trigger but Jess had her head back, eyes closed, panting hard, and she was still spasming around his dick, squeezing him like a boa, with tight hard contractions. Sweat sheened her face and chest giving her a well-satisfied glow.

Her heart was pounding so hard, he could see the shimmy of her breasts with each beat. Colin's heart pounded equally hard in double time. For a moment he thought he'd gone deaf and dumb. He couldn't hear anything but the overpowering thud in his ears and all sensation was focused on her wet fist holding his cock so tightly he never wanted to leave.

"Fuck." Colin dropped his forehead against the curve of her neck.

He was still holding her up against the wall. His arms were starting to shake with the effort, not because she was heavy but because he was so wrecked from the mind-blowing orgasm she'd just given him. But he didn't want to let her go.

"Oui, monsieur," she replied coquettishly.

"You are amazing," he said loudly. Colin pressed a kiss to her neck and murmured. "I hope your brother never sees this tape, or I'm history."

"Merci, monsieur." Then she breathed in his ear, "None of his business."

"Hopefully I managed to shield most of you from the cameras."

Jess jerked back a little. Then she took one hand from his shoulders and gripped his hair in her fist. She jerked his head toward her and took his mouth in a carnal kiss. She devoured him, inhaled him, and destroyed him with the sheer power of her mouth. She hadn't realized what he'd been trying to do. Her thanks was doing fantastic things to him.

As if electricity shot from the fingertips she held against his jaw, a current sizzled straight to his cock. He was getting hard again. He hadn't even gone completely soft from one of the most explosive orgasms of his life and he was getting ready to go again.

"You are so...eager, monsieur." She giggled, but it was the fake one. "But first we must freshen up from this last encounter."

Perfect. She had segued them right into a need to find a bathroom. And gave him the opportunity to get 'lost' in the halls.

The earth trembled and the room rocked slightly. "Aftershock." Another harder, longer trembler struck. This was perfect. They could use the fear of the occupants to deliver the poison and the ensuing chaos to get the hell out of here.

"Give me the stuff." He nuzzled her ear as he demanded.

"Non."

"If I get caught, it's not that big of a deal. He needs the money and the aid." But if she were to get caught, the consequences would be severe. No one was going to notice if one woman went missing after a natural disaster. However, the executive officer of a relief org that gave the President money went missing, it would create an incident that LeRoy couldn't afford.

"We do it together." She rebutted. "You can do the actual deed," she avoided the word, poison. "If it makes you feel better, but you need a lookout."

Colin's stomach cramped. He knew that from their conversations six months ago that she was conflicted. He didn't want her to compromise her principles.

Jack had made him promise not to pressure her. That way she could make an informed decision. And if she chose not to participate in the deadly part of the mission, her conscience would be intact. She could continue to work for Jack on strictly the humanitarian side. He'd had Colin head this mission so that she would bear no ill will toward her brothers if she chose to back out. But now Colin was more worried about protecting her than protecting Jack and the company. "What about your...issues?"

"After the suffering we saw today, how can he live with himself?" she argued quietly. "I'm good."

Colin looked at her. Really looked.

Her hair was mussed, her pale skin flushed with the aftereffects of explosive sex and the sizzle of excitement. Her green eyes were bright with anticipation. Adrenaline had visibly affected her. She was getting off on the whole situation. The adrenaline. The danger. She was better than good. She was pumped.

He dove in for one last carnal kiss. Jess let her legs slide down his body, feeling liquid yet humming with tension. "Let us find a bathroom cherie and we can go for round two."

They slipped into the hallway. Colin had to hope LeRoy wouldn't leave his guests alone in the main ballroom. He needed to schmooze as many people as possible. And hopefully that last aftershock had created a little chaos.

And Colin wasn't about to leave her behind. How could he? She wanted to be here. She was the one who came up with the plan.

She caressed his shoulder with affection, 'be careful' inherent in the light touch. And then they walked out. "Let's do this."

Jack Stone was going to kill him dead. Colin's lips curved as he remembered the sound Jess made when he slid home. The little moan that was more than a puff of breath but less than a full scream. A reminiscent smile curved his lips and right this second, he couldn't bring himself to care.

Of course, that wasn't really true. He was blowing a years' long friendship and a mutually respectful professional relationship by ignoring Jack's request. But there was something about Jess. He hadn't been able to resist her.

Fuck, he was a dead man.

wo weeks later

"Jessica!" Jack roared from his office. Ava, his assistant froze, one elegantly-manicured hand on her throat, the other wrapped around the waist of her Calvin Klein suit.

Since Jess was almost at his door, the annoyed shout was completely unnecessary.

In the week since she had returned, her relationship with Jack had steadily improved. She finally felt as if she were truly a part of the family business. But the thunderous look on his face shot her straight back to outsider.

Dammit. Jess's mood plummeted. She needed this job for more reasons than one. She'd returned from Port-du-Bois buoyed by her success in the field. LeRoy had been found dead, apparently died in his sleep, so their mission had worked. Antoine D'Aramitz, with full support from the military, had stepped in. The deplorable conditions for the people of Port-du-Bois had improved almost overnight. The change in leadership occurred without bloodshed and at little to no cost to the devastated citizens who needed help, not an embezzling immoral leader.

Justice had been served Stone cold.

After the off the cuff, last minute change in plans, Jess had earned Keisha's grudging respect. Jess still didn't know why Keisha acted the way she did but they had reached a tentative peace, and Keisha had actually invited her to lunch yesterday.

Jess was thrilled about her newly changed, closer relationship with her brother Jack. When she'd asked him why he hadn't told her the truth about GHR and Stone Consulting, that the organization had multi-faceted layers of involvement in the countries and situations they participated in, he'd responded, "Sink or swim, baby. You are our sister. I was pretty damn sure that you'd step up to the action. But if you didn't or couldn't, this was the perfect opportunity to test the waters. And you performed, came through with flying colors, even better than I could have imagined."

Her sense of pride was nearly overwhelming when Jack said, "Welcome to the family biz, sweetheart."

She fit at GHR. She finally realized she could do good and still utilize her other skills when necessary. She was vital to the organization. It was as if everything was just falling into place.

Except for one thing. The only area of her life that was not going well was her heart. She had known her interlude with Colin would be brief, explosive and over before they left Port-du-Bois but even so, she hadn't anticipated the speed and finality of the end.

They'd managed to get the poison into LeRoy's bathroom without getting caught. There had been a few

hairy moments. She'd had to duck into a hall closet when her guard pal almost caught up with her.

Aftershocks had continued to rock the city and they made their way back to the camp without detection. The soldiers were too busy trying to control the panicked citizens who were totally freaked out. The streets had been packed with terrified people afraid once again to go back inside.

Even though it had been late and most of the relief workers were tucked away in their tents, the occasional emergency siren blew long and loud. And when they'd gotten back to the compound, Colin had thanked her stiffly for her commitment to the cause and then promptly sent her to her own tent.

The only conversations they'd had after that pertained strictly to their relief work.

So two weeks later, even after full days of satisfying work, she went home every night to her lonely condo and she relived the moments with Colin.

Not just the sex, although, who was she kidding, she definitely missed how he made her feel. But she missed his company too. She'd missed him.

She refused to mope. He was clearly treating their time in Port-du-Bois as a hook up. She hadn't heard from him since she got back to Monterey. And she knew he was in town. The entire office had been buzzing about the handsome, hot Brit.

Jess shoved into Jack's office. "What's got your panties in a twist?" She flipped her hair over her shoulder and simultaneously noticed Colin sitting in the chair in front of Jack's desk. His familiar light brown hair and heart-jerking tilt of his head hit her. And then he turned around and looked straight at her spearing her heart with his direct regard. Jack tossed a glossy picture on his desk but Jess couldn't tear her gaze from Colin.

Wonderful.

She hoped she was hiding her visceral reaction to being in the same room with Colin again. But she wasn't sure. She licked her lips and tore her gaze from her former lover as Jack burst up from his chair, fists clenched and his dark black hair standing on end.

"What. The. Hell?" He snarled.

Colin jumped up from his chair and placed himself between Jess and Jack. She gave him a strange look. "What are you doing?"

Colin jerked his chin at her brother. "Protecting you."

Jess fell back a step. "Jack wouldn't hurt me." At least not physically.

"But I would hurt you." Jack stepped around his desk and fists in the air, threw a punch at Colin.

Colin's head snapped back but he didn't lift his hands to protect himself. A trail of blood trickled from the corner of his mouth. He wiggled his jaw back and forth a few times but didn't say a word.

"Jack!"

Jack punched Colin again. "Are you such a man-whore that you couldn't keep it in your pants for a few weeks?"

Jess's face drained of color. "What?" she whispered.

"Are you such an ass that you would bring it up in front of your sister?" Colin snapped back.

"It's been brought up in front of a hell of a lot more people than my sister, since I was sent the photos to prove it," Jack said viciously.

"Photos?" Jess said faintly. There must have been surveillance in that room. At the time, she hadn't cared. But standing in her brother's office, she was re-thinking that nonchalance.

Colin picked the 8 x 10 picture up off of Jack's desk. "It's my ass hanging out," he said casually.

Jess peered over Colin's shoulder and winced. Awesome. Even though only part of her face was visible, her bare legs were wrapped around Colin's very fine ass, and she was clearly identifiable in the picture.

It looked like Colin was showing her a very good time. Her head was thrown back and her mouth was curved in ecstasy.

"She did the job," Colin said to Jack. "She used her head and found a way in to the mansion to get the poison to me."

"And you just couldn't resist using her too?" Jack clenched his fists as if he was going to hit Colin again.

"The picture evidence would support our decision to make it real," Colin replied wearily. "If they'd had any suspicion after observing us in that room, we both, or at the very least, Jess would be dead."

All very valid, logical reasons. But suddenly Jess was back in that guest room. And she knew that the picture revealed a whole other reason for the fact that they'd had sex in that room. Their desire practically leapt from that photo. Sensual, sultry, and totally hot.

"Jack." Suddenly, Jess's temper began to boil. "If Keisha and Colin had sex in Port-du-Bois, this would be a non-issue. So why are you giving Colin a hard time?"

"Because I asked him to keep it in his pants. He was supposed to be watching over you, not boning you."

"You...." Her anger hit white hot. "Are you serious? I'm twenty-eight years old. It's not like I'm in high school and getting pressure from the Homecoming King, for God's sake."

"You're still my baby sister."

Jess rolled her eyes. "I cannot believe this."

Jack wasn't finished. "He promised me—"

"I'm sorry," Colin said stiffly. "I apologize for betraying our friendship."

He turned on his heel and walked toward the door.

Jack yelled, "What were you thinking?"

Colin spun around. "Jess has a joy that is incandescent. I just...wanted her to warm me up. How do you not see it?" Colin jabbed his finger at Jack. His usually pale eyes were dark with repressed emotion and his face almost angry. "Wouldn't you do whatever it took to feel that alive, that satisfied?"

Silence filled the office.

Jack's face was a mask of stunned remorse. "Jesus," he whispered. "You weren't just boning her."

"No, you idiot." Colin said despairingly, "I couldn't bear to stay away from her."

Jess was stunned. Her feet rooted to the floor as a gaping hole opened in her chest and all his longing and sorrow poured in filling her up. She stood unmoving, as Colin stalked toward the door and away from her.

"What are you doing?" Jack whispered. "Go after him."

She was frozen, numb. The seething emotion coming from Colin had taken her completely by surprise. She had made the decision six months ago to take control of her life. Take control of her future. She'd mostly been thinking of her career and her family life. But suddenly she realized she needed to take control of her *life.*

"Wait." Jess sprinted toward him and grabbed Colin's bicep. He was hard and tense underneath her palm. She realized she'd fit with him since that hot, close room in a dingy underground station. They fit.

Colin turned, his face completely impassive. If she hadn't seen his intensity a minute ago, she would have thought that he could care less.

"You think I have that—"

"I know you do," Colin interrupted.

"Let me finish," Jess snapped. Her heart was beating so hard, she thought she might pass out. This was so important. She had to say it right. "I don't. Whatever you see, whatever you feel with me, is because of you."

Colin shook his head.

"It's true," Jess insisted, sick at his misery. "You do that to me. We fit."

She skimmed her hand over his hair. She'd clearly shocked him. As if he couldn't bear not to touch her any longer, Colin curled his hard fingers around her shoulders and yanked her against his hard, familiar body.

Jess melted against him. "I missed you," she whispered in his ear.

He slid his arms around her back and held her tight. "I missed you too."

"It sorta seems impossible." People didn't fall that fast. Did they?

"I've been missing you for the last six months." Colin slid a hand up the back of her neck and cupped her head. "But the last two weeks have been torture."

Oh, she melted just a little bit more. How did such a hard ass say the sweetest things? She nudged his erection with the curve of her belly, equally as turned on but they had things to discuss first.

What did he really mean? "What are we talking here?" Jess wasn't leaving anything in uncertain terms. She'd made the decision to go after life. If she was going to go after it, she was going all the way.

"A shot at making this," he pressed light sucking kisses along her jawline. "Work." And then he took her mouth. There was no other way to describe the possessive, dominating power of his kiss. He attacked as if his ship was going down and he refused to surrender.

Jess broke away from the kiss and rested her forehead against Colin's. She gazed into his intense, gray eyes. "We've got some logistics to work out."

Jack cleared his throat.

A hot blush spread over her face. She'd completely forgotten that her brother was still in the room.

"Why are you still here?" Colin growled.

Jack's voice was the tiniest bit amused as he replied, "Because it's my office."

Colin kissed her again and nudged her toward the door. "Let's discuss this somewhere more private."

Jess reveled in the hard circle of his arms and the sensual press of his body against hers. "Sounds good to me."

Jack cleared his throat again. "If you two stop making out in front of me, I might have a solution."

"Is it wrong of me to want to shoot your brother right now?"

Jess snorted. "I am pretty skilled with a pistol, I can show you how."

"Brilliant." Colin smiled against her mouth and pressed her up against the office wall. "If we ignore him maybe he'll go away."

"I thought I'd offer you a job, you ungrateful Brit," Jack said without an ounce of anger. "Just so we're clear, I had planned to do this before I saw the picture of you two."

"What do you think?" Jess held her breath. Working

together was tricky. Of course, they'd managed it in Port-du-Bois under fairly extreme circumstances.

"I'm up for it."

Jess snickered. "You're up for more than that."

"Oh God, my eyes," Jack murmured. Right before he shut the door, he begged, "Just please don't have sex on my desk."

They ignored him.

EPILOGUE

on

"Connor!"

Connor Stone's oldest brother, Jack, yelled through the doorway of his office. The sound traveled all the way down the hall and through Con's closed door.

Con yanked his door open and stomped toward the reception area and Jack's office. "Jesus, Jack." He swiped a fall of blond hair from his eyes as he strode past Ava, Jack's assistant. Con steeled himself to greet her casually with a quick smile, an informal wave, keeping his tone and demeanor low-key so that she would have no idea how much he wanted her. "Hey, Ava."

"Hello, Connor," she replied softly as he barged into Jack's office. Peripherally, he noted her conservative, trim red suit and matching fingernails. The lush contours of her smoking hot body were hidden beneath the staid boxy clothes. Not that he should be noticing her body, but hell he was a guy.

He breathed a quick sigh of relief as he successfully managed to make it past her without revealing any of the lust that he felt. She was Jack's assistant and therefore totally off limits. Plus he was pretty sure he made her nervous.

"What the hell is your deal?" Con's suppressed desire made his voice sharper than he intended.

"I need you."

Con tried not to let the words mean too much but he could feel his chest swell and his throat get a little tight. He was still trying to live down his wild, out-of-control teenage past, even though he was twenty-eight years old and had retired from the Army after seven years and multiple tours. "What for?"

"Close the door for a sec."

Con shut the door and raised his blond eyebrows. Jack shifted in his massive desk chair and flattened his lips. He hadn't seen Jack this out of sorts since the day that Jess and Shelley, their half-sister and her mother, had come to live with them at the Stone Mansion twenty years ago. Their bastard of a father, Jackson Stone Senior, told the whole family Jack was the man of the house and promptly left. Jack had been fourteen.

Con stood in front of Jack's desk, military stiff, feet apart, hands clasped behind his back in parade rest.

"At ease, soldier." Jack chuckled. "While I love the fact that you consider me like your commanding Lord and Master—"

Con snorted. His brother always knew how to push it.

"You're out of the Army now," Jack continued. "There's no need for military protocol in the office."

But the military had given him the structure he needed

and the discipline to become a better version of himself. Con shrugged. "I'm comfortable with it," he said simply.

Jack's moment of amusement was gone, replaced by a somber frown. "Okay. I have to be out of the office for a few days. Unfortunately."

"So do you need intel for your trip?"

"No." If anything his frown got deeper. "That part is taken care of."

Jack stared off into the distance, his face a mask of grumpiness and annoyance. He rubbed a hand over his mouth and shook his head to clear whatever had taken root in his mind. Con thought he saw a flash of worry in Jack's eyes but he knew that wasn't right. Nothing scared Jack. He was the ultimate protector, the ultimate big brother, and the head of their family since the age of fourteen. Damn their irresponsible father.

"Muscle?" Con asked with bemusement. That seemed unlikely. Jack could take care of himself.

Another smile quirked Jack's mouth. "Pretty sure of yourself, aren't you?"

About some things, yes. About lots of others, not a chance. But he wasn't about to share that with Jack.

"It's a Stone Consulting job," Jack clarified. "Classified."

They'd all had jobs that had been classified at one time or another, except for Ava Sanchez. Jack had hired her straight out of college from Cal State Monterey Bay. She'd been with Jack since the beginning of GHR and Stone Consulting. Con knew her degree was in global studies with a concentration in nongovernment organizations— not that he'd happened to read her personnel file or anything—and that she never quite looked him in the eyes.

"I really need your help on a separate job." Jack stared out the reflective glass window, the view of the Monterey

Bay obscured by lingering morning fog. Wisps of clouds drifted lazily in the gray sky.

Connor tried not to let Jack's words raise his hopes. Usually his contribution to the company was relegated to light hacking, keeping both companies' firewalls intact, and muscle when they needed an extra body on an op. But now, Jack needed his help?

Con stayed silent. He had no idea where Jack was going with this. When Connor just waited patiently, Jack finally said, "You can get so quiet it's freaky. How are we even related?"

And there it was. Connor's reminder that he wasn't like the other Stone siblings. He wasn't the oldest, he wasn't the charmer, he wasn't the sister. Hell he didn't even look like his brothers and sister. They had dark hair and green or hazel eyes while Con was blond with a really weird mix of brown and gold eyes.

He was the leftover. The extra. His father had reminded him of that fact often enough growing up. When he was a teenager he'd grabbed attention by acting out, being crazy. Fortunately the Army cured him of that habit. Now he had one motto: *Deeds not words*.

Con had to play it calm. *Deeds not words.* He was finally being given the chance to show that he wasn't the same crazy, spoiled boy that Jack heard about after he left home.

"Can you run an intensive background check on José Fernandez?"

"Sure." Connor waited for more information, wondering why that name sounded familiar. "Am I looking for anything specific?"

"I don't know." Jack rubbed his finger along his scarred eyebrow. He'd never confessed how he had scarred it but Con had enough experience in the Army to know that a bullet had come way too close to his brother's brain. "I need anything and everything you can find on the guy. There's got to be something there, even if no one has found it yet. I don't want to influence your search, so I'm keeping it vague. But I believe he is dirty."

Connor's interest was piqued. A puzzle. "You got it. Anything else?"

"Don't tell anyone what you are working on."

Con shrugged. That wouldn't be a problem.

"Stay here a sec." Jack pressed the intercom on his phone. "Ava, my office now."

Con jerked. He tried to avoid being in small enclosed spaces with her. "You want me to leave?" He hoped his tone wasn't as desperate as he was feeling.

For whatever reason, the last few weeks he'd had more trouble than usual avoiding her. And every time he saw her, his heart rate soared and his thoughts went increasingly to pictures of them together. Not that he would ever do anything about those pictures. He had changed, matured, and he wasn't going to destroy his newfound image by getting busy with an employee.

"No. I still need you here."

Ava opened the door and hurried to the office entrance.

"Yes?" She hovered half in, half out of the doorway. Connor cut a quick glance her way but she was completely focused on Jack. She never said much, even though he knew she spoke four different languages. She was efficient, organized, had the proper attitude and mindset for the Global Humanitarian Relief, and probably didn't know everything they did at GHR's subsidiary, Stone Consulting.

"I'm going out of town. And I've got some instructions for you." Jack tapped the blotter on his desk. "And Connor."

Jack waited one more second and then said, "I'm leaving Connor in charge of the office."

"Me?" And damn if Con's voice didn't rise slightly like a prepubescent boy getting asked out by the hottest girl in school.

"Yeah, you," Jack said as if putting Con in charge made perfect sense. "Riley is delivering books and school supplies to Sulu Island in the Philippines. Jess and Colin are in England until next Tuesday getting his stuff ready to move here. I have to go out of town and I want a Stone in charge."

Jack's brow lifted, as if trying to impart some silent message, but Con was too distracted to interpret that look. Con could care less what the message was. This was a huge step.

A fierce sense of pride flooded him. Jack was entrusting GHR, his personal baby, to Con. But he'd take that out and examine it later. Right now he needed to focus on logistics. "How long are you going to be gone?"

"I don't know." Jack continued tapping the pen. "And I don't know what my comm options will be so I may be out of cell reach for some of my trip."

Con wondered at the lack of information. Jack didn't seem to be trying to be intentionally vague. If anything he seemed irritated and out of sorts. Con tilted his head, waiting for more info. But Jack didn't answer his unspoken question.

"Ava, is there anything hot right now?"

"Just the situation with Riley." Her husky voice scraped over Connor's spine like a lover's fingernails over his naked back, and his body responded accordingly. Hell, this was why he tried to avoid her.

"So you're on." Jack pointed at Con. But then he got one last dig in by cautioning, "Don't fuck it up."

Connor's good humor deflated faster than a parachute canopy after a flare. *Thanks for the vote of confidence, bro.* But he didn't say the words out loud. Couldn't. He'd always be the youngest, no value added, just some leftover kid that ended up living with the Stone family, related by birth but that's it. Sometimes he wondered why he'd ever come to work for Jack.

"And no having sex on my desk."

THANK you for reading Jess and Colin's story. I hope you enjoyed reading Stone Cold Heart as much as I enjoyed writing it!

WANT to know whether Connor and Ava act on their mutual attraction or follow Jack's order? One-click CARVED IN STONE now!

p.s. Would you like to know when my next book is available? You can sign up for my new release email list/newsletter at Lisa's Confidants

Ava Sanchez scurried toward her desk and cursed her tendency to blush. Luckily, with her swarthy skin tone and her current healthy tan—she'd spent a decent amount of time at the beach this summer—her blush likely wasn't *too* noticeable. However, she couldn't completely hide her deep embarrassment. When Jack had issued his 'no sex on the desk' command, she'd had no chance to temper her reaction. It was as if he'd reached right into her favorite fantasy and blurted it out to Connor.

She sighed. Connor, who never even noticed her.

Oh, he acknowledged her. He smiled. Said hello. But he never really *looked* at her. And maybe on the outside she appeared as a confident, well-dressed, well-groomed woman, but on the inside she was still that painfully shy wallflower, the migrant worker who didn't quite belong, who squeaked when spoken to and couldn't ever act normal in a social situation.

She'd worked hard to overcome her natural reticence. To learn to be polished and to strive for classy and sophisticated. To eradicate the dust and dirt from the fields and her native Sinaloan accent. She'd come a long way in the last eight years, but she still had difficulty speaking to men she found attractive. And she definitely found Connor Stone attractive.

"Sorry, Ava," Jack called from his office. She knew he was. He was gruff and a little rough around the edges but he meant well. He'd given her a job right out of college and helped her acclimate to a new world with affection and patience. He treated all his employees like family, which meant he frequently didn't think before he spoke.

Jack, she could handle. She grinned. "Expect my lawsuit in the mail," she quipped back, completely at ease with her totally hot boss. And he was. Totally hot. At thirty-four, he was also a little on the old side for her. But Ava wasn't attracted to Jack. He didn't make her girl parts tingle the way his brother did. Jack was like the older brother she'd never had and always wanted.

Jack gave a shout of laughter.

Why had Jack said that? Could he know that she frequently daydreamed about the youngest Stone brother? All the other women in the office were *loco* over Riley. And no doubt Riley was extremely handsome, smooth, and very charming. He always made her feel feminine and special. But he did that to everyone. Ava preferred the quiet confidence and the understated smarts of Connor Stone.

He was physically intimidating, as big as Jack and definitely as muscular. Since she wasn't a simpering skinny swizzle stick, but a solid woman with more curves than she'd like and the build of a peasant, Ava appreciated Connor's bulk. She imagined that he would make her feel delicate and dainty if he wrapped his solid, massive biceps around her and cupped her ass in his large palms.

"Hey." Connor stood in front of her desk.

Ava jerked and blinked up at him. She could feel an even deeper flush thunder through her body like a wave of heat. Great, while she'd been daydreaming, he'd been watching her imagine him naked and wrapped around her. "Er. Hello."

"Ignore him. He's an idiot."

"Okay. Thanks."

And if only he'd shut up then, because that was the perfect place to stop. Instead, he kept going. "Of course we aren't going to...."

Of course. Because no way could a guy that good looking, that smart, that *everything*, ever want to have sex with her. Ava's temper began to simmer. "Of course not." Her snide tone left no room for interpretation.

Connor looked very uncomfortable as he figured out that he'd just insulted her. "Uhhh, I don't think that came out the way I meant it."

And like that she boiled over. "How did you mean it?" she said sweetly, softly. She blinked at him with her most innocent, wide-eyed, non-threatening expression for the first time truly looking him in the eyes. He had gorgeous eyes, a sunburst of caramel, chocolate and a hint of pale green in a kaleidescope of color. Tawny, gold, predatory.

He was a very smart man. And he'd figured out that no matter what he said, he was trapped and going to offend her. Like the very smart man he was, Connor backed away. "I meant no disrespect."

If that was the way he wanted to leave it. "Fine."

That stereotypical Latina temper was a stereotype for a reason but she usually left her hothead reactions at the door. She needed this job and most importantly, she wanted this job to atone for the past. It was a bonus that she loved working here. She loved that she was using her degree but also doing some good. GHR was the perfect vehicle for her need to do penance. For her luck in surviving when Maria...Maria hadn't.

"Ava...."

He wasn't going to go away until she forgave him for the insult and let him off the hook. Too bad she didn't want to forgive him.

"Sure. None taken," Ava said dismissively, clearly lying. She purposely stared down at her monitor and started typing away. Too bad she had no idea what document was open or what she was typing. If he looked at the screen, he would only see gibberish.

Connor stood in front of her desk, arms hanging limply at his sides, half-turned toward Jack's office, half-facing her, as if undecided about what to do next.

She continued to pretend that she was ultra-busy, praying he would go away so that she could run to the bathroom and compose herself. She could hear Jack on the phone in his office, arranging the company jet to be at the Monterey regional airport. Soon.

Jack didn't sound happy. And she wondered why he was doing his own scheduling rather than having her take care of it. There was plenty of work that he took care of himself already. But he always had her schedule their pilot, Shane, and make the travel arrangements.

Connor hadn't left the area by her desk and his presence was beginning to make her sweat. She wondered if Connor was going to use Jack's office while Jack was gone, and if so, how was she going to get any work done with him less than fifty feet away and always just...there? She'd be a distracted mess the entire time.

Out of the corner of her eye, she noted his feet had started moving.

Only he wasn't leaving. He was stalking toward her, literally like a leopard toward its prey. Finally, all she could see was his thick, muscular thighs and the intriguing bulge in his crotch, covered by tan cargo pants, before he slammed his hands down on her desk, his blunt fingers and wide palms flattened on top of the report she was supposed to be typing.

His biceps rippled as he leaned close, his broad solid torso loomed over her and Ava fought the urge to lean away from the clear menace in Connor's pose. "Let's get one thing perfectly straight," he said softly, his face was set in fierce lines, and his multi-colored eyes glowed with fiery intensity.

Ava hypnotically lifted her gaze to his face, overwhelmed by his sheer physical presence. Arousal tingled through her at his proximity and his obvious strength. "Just because I won't, doesn't mean I don't *want*."

Connor shoved up and off her desk, then strode purposefully away. Ava was struck speechless by his words as she watched the play of his glutes beneath his snug cargo pants. Her heart still beat erratically in her chest and either she'd had a major sugar crash from her hard boiled egg breakfast or all the blood in her head had rushed south to a very under-used body part.

One question kept circling in her suddenly light-headed brain: Did he just say he wanted *her*?

Riley Stone didn't have a *type*.

He loved all women equally. Short, Tall, Skinny, Round. Outgoing. Shy. Young. Old. Sweet. Sexy. Surly.

And they loved him right back.

When he was younger, he'd come to the very happy conclusion, that he could charm his way out of, or sometimes into, any touchy situation.

He'd developed the skill as a young kid. When he'd realized that he was never going to be a good reader, or a good student, he'd made the decision that he'd have to rely on his other attributes. He could charm his grades up from any teacher in whose class he might need a little help. Which came in handy when he knew he wasn't going to pass a test.

He made it a point to always have something nice to say. As an adult, charming people was second nature. He didn't even have to think about doing it.

When he grew up, he finally understood that his talent was in making people feel better about themselves and better in general. How he approached a situation might vary from person to person, but if using a little charm eased the way, he was gonna use it.

He was shallow enough to use his God given talent to charm women into bed, at least he had been. These days he was more focused on making a go of GHR and Stone Consulting with his brothers and sister than in scoring with a hot woman.

But he still couldn't help himself when it came to charming people, especially women.

"How's it going, sweetheart?" He stopped to chat with Ava Sanchez, his brother Jack's assistant, making her blush and stammer. She was a complete hottie and didn't even seem to realize it. But Riley's Rules Number Ten: Never do more than lightly flirt with co-workers.

He'd managed to maintain an amicable relationship with every woman he'd ever had a thing with. It was a particular point of pride with him. But odds were, at some time, things wouldn't end well. And he'd never jeopardize a working relationship, or Global Humanitarian Relief and Stone Consulting, which meant sweet Ava was off limits.

He smiled gently at her. "He ready for me?"

"Yes. You can go on in," she replied with a tilt of her head. "He's got company."

"Client?"

She nodded, lowered her lashes and smiled.

"Okay." Riley paused to adjust the cuffs of his Egyptian cotton dress shirt and smooth his hand down his bright, geometric Jhane Barnes tie. He made it a point to be well-dressed in the office in case there were meetings with clients. It was rare but it did happen. From his vantage point in the doorway, he could see the woman in Jack's office. He didn't recognize her from the back. She seemed delicate, the curve of her head covered with a riot of short blond curls but her body language screamed supreme annoyance.

Riley curved his lips into a casual smile and sauntered into Jack's office. His big gruff brother seemed to be conversing carefully with the woman across from him.

Jack looked up and the hard set of his shoulders relaxed. "Ry, you're here." A desperate smile lit his face as he stood and grabbed Riley's hand like a lifeline. "I'd like you to meet, Diana Lundberg from *Tools for Schools*."

The woman stood abruptly and shoved out her hand in a very masculine move to greet him.

She was tall, more sleek lines and hard angles than soft curves but when her hard, capable fingers curled around his much larger palm, Riley took a serious punch to the gut. Lust hit, hard and unexpected, as he grasped her far more delicate fingers and gazed into her wary, pale blue eyes.

"Pleasure," he finally murmured dazedly.

She tugged her hand from his and turned to Jack. "*He's* going to take TFS into the jungle?" Her curved brow was derisive and her tone bordered on insolent.

Jack leapt to Riley's defense. "He's extremely well-trained and has knowledge of the area."

"I'm a lot more adaptable than I look." Riley smiled seductively, unable to stop the flow of innuendo. He wanted her. Bad. He carefully put his hands in his pockets to stop the instinctive need to reach out and grab her hand again. He hated to do it as it ruined the line of his fine wool gabardine trousers but desperate times and desperate measures needed to be taken. It wouldn't do to accost the client.

She snorted. "I'm sure."

Her abrasive attitude was starting to drill into the haze

of attraction he had running through him. "Where am I headed?"

"Philippines," Jack clipped out. "Sulu, specifically."

Great. He'd had plenty of experience in country. Not his favorite as the political climate sucked almost as bad as the weather this time of year. Monsoon season was just about over, but the weather didn't always conform to the timetables put out by man. Not to mention the bugs. He shuddered. But he would deal. "Cargo?"

"School supplies," Jack replied.

"Piece of cake." Riley grinned, exposed his white teeth and tried to put her at ease. But he got lost in the magnetism she exuded like a force field even as he noted peripherally the angry vibe that radiated from her.

But angry babe wasn't put at ease. If anything, she stiffened even further, as her pale eyes shot sparks at him. "*I* am going to the Philippines. I am not so sure about you."

But Riley had stopped listening at *I*.

"Wait, what?" His eyebrows rose and he snapped his head toward Jack. He straightened from his nonchalant slouch and snatched his hands from his pockets. "You can't possibly expect me to take her," he gestured, careful to keep his voice low-key and well-modulated. "To Sulu Island."

A rosy flush of annoyance spread across her high delicate cheekbones as she pursed her pale pink lips and her body vibrated with a fine tension.

"Exactly," Di said. She dismissed Riley with a disdainful sweep of her lashes and trained her gaze on Jack. "Who else do you have?"

ACKNOWLEDGMENTS

No writer works in a vacuum. I am very fortunate to have a supportive group of writers and professionals behind me.

Huge thanks to Adrienne Bell, LGC Smith, and Cecilia Gray for pretty much everything and anything. A special shout out to Adrienne Bell for the ongoing word wars!! The Pens for being totally awesome-sauce, whether it be emergency pick-me-ups, or writing retreats at the haunted house, or impromptu sessions at Panera, or lunches at Buffalo Hot Wings.

To LJ at Mayhem Cover Creations. Thank you, thank you for the beautiful covers!
Thank you all. :)

<u>Cold as Stone (John, Family Stone #7)</u>

<u>Family Stone Box Set (Stone Cold Heart, Carved in Stone, Heart of Stone, Still the One, & Jar of Hearts)</u>

<u>The Nostradamus Prophecies</u>

<u>View To A Kill #1</u>

Never Say Never #2

<u>ALIAS</u>

Stalked (ALIAS #1)

Hunted (ALIAS #2)

Vanished (ALIAS #3)

Deceived (ALIAS #4)

<u>Billionaire Breakfast Club</u>

His Semi-Charmed Life (Camp Firefly Falls #11 and Billionaire Breakfast Club #0)

Everything He Wants (Billionaire Breakfast Club #1 The Jock)

Queen of His Daydreams (Camp Firefly Falls #23 and Billionaire Breakfast Club #1.5)

USA Today Bestselling Author Lisa Hughey started writing romance in the fourth grade. That particular story involved a prince and an engagement. Now, she writes about strong heroines who are perfectly capable of rescuing themselves and the heroes who love both their strength and their vulnerability. She pens romances of all types—suspense, paranormal, and contemporary—but at their heart, all her books celebrate the power of love.

She lives in Cape Ann Massachusetts with her fabulously supportive husband, two out of three awesome mostly-grown kids, and one somewhat grumpy cat.

Beach walks, hiking, and traveling are her favorite ways to pass the time when she isn't plotting new ways to get her characters to fall in love.

Lisa loves to hear from readers and has tons of places you can connect with her. It's a wonder she gets any writing done at all….

Sign Up for Lisa's Confidants
Visit Lisa on the Web

Follow Lisa's Boards on Pinterest
Follow Lisa on Instagram
Email Lisa
Be Lisa's Friend on Goodreads
Like Lisa on Facebook at Lisa Hughey: My Books